FINDING COOPER

Once Upon a Funeral

ELLE WRIGHT

Finding Cooper

Paperback ISBN: 978-0-9994213-7-6

Elle Wrights Books, LLC
Ypsilanti, Michigan
www.ElleWright.com
Editor:
Nicole Falls
Trim and Polish

Cover Design:
Sherelle Green

Finding Cooper

When the powerful patriarch of the Prescott family dies, four brothers are challenged to return to Rosewood Heights and fulfill their grandfather's last wishes. With each of these compelling and complex men facing their inner demons, they must ask themselves if light can shine in the midst of tragedy and if home is truly where the heart is...

Cooper Prescott... Strong. Hot-tempered. A charming rebel protége in every way. He may be content with keeping his life the same, however, fate is a beast that always has the last say.

Dear Reader

I love a good Anthology! And I adore working with my lit sisters, Angela, Sherelle, and Sheryl!

I fell in love with Cooper, Angel, and Mehki! This was such an emotional, yet rewarding journey for me. But I LOVED it! I hope you enjoy the ride.

Love,

Elle

www.ellewright.com

For my Granddad Harry-O! I miss you so much!

Game Changer

COOPER

It's time. Come home.

For at least the fiftieth time today, I stared at my phone. The message from my text-averse grandfather stared back at me. Although I'd received it four hours ago, I still hadn't responded because the deep part of me worried he wouldn't answer. Yet, his words were a clear warning, a plea.

My thumb hovered over my phone, ready to call my sister, Ava, to ask about Granddad's status. Admittedly, I sucked. Since we'd gotten the news that there were only mere weeks left in his life, I could count the visits home I'd taken on one hand. The bone cancer had transformed the biggest person in my world to a shell of his former, powerful self.

Abraham Theodore Prescott had always been larger than life, amassing wealth that few African American men had in his time. Prescott Holdings was a multi-million dollar empire with dozens of money-making resorts and casinos under its control. The man who'd built the corporation was withering away in a hospital bed, wracked in pain, consumed by morphine and other medicine designed to keep him comfortable. The only man who'd encouraged me to see the world, to give back to those in need, to not let my father construct my life, would soon be gone. And I was too much of a coward to say goodbye.

Sighing, I dialed Ava. When she answered, I couldn't speak. So she did.

"Coop?" Her voice was shaky, like she'd been crying. "He's not dead."

Relieved, I closed my eyes. I could hear people in the background and the faint sounds of oxygen and heart monitors.

"He perked up this morning, though," she continued. "Asked for a full breakfast, and to use his phone. Everyone is happy, hopeful." Her voice broke. "He asked about you. He wants to see you."

My schedule was clear, but I knew I didn't want my last memory of the man who'd molded me, pushed me, and accepted me to be of him lying in a hospital bed struggling to breathe. "I can't make it," I lied.

"Please?" Ava whispered.

My only sister had a reputation of being tough as nails in business, a woman never to be trifled with or talked down to. Although she was the youngest sibling, of the five of us, she was the strongest. Faced with the imminent death of our grandfather, though, she'd cracked. I'd recognized it on the many calls, the few video chats, and during the short visit to Rosewood Heights, South Carolina I'd made last month—after the holidays, right before the New Year. So I could slip in and out without any expectations.

Hearing her so wrecked brought out the protective, big brother in me.

"Coop, I need you here," she pleaded.

Again, my little sister pulled at my heart strings. "Ava, I can't…" I swallowed. "I can't see him like that."

"Even if it's what he wants?" she asked.

"Shit," I grumbled. "Okay. I'll get there today. Right now, I'm at the courthouse."

"Courthouse? Wh-Why?"

"No comment." I glanced up in time to see my friend and attorney approaching. Without breaking eye contact from my lawyer, I said, "I have to go, sis. I'll talk to you later."

"But, Coop, I—"

I ended the call.

Before I could greet the woman who would soon save my life, she snatched my cold cup of coffee from my hand and tossed it in a nearby trashcan. "I'm charging you a premium for this bullshit," she said, smoothing a hand down her skirt. "You do realize I had a flight booked to a tropical, all-inclusive haven that had to cancel for your stupidity?"

"I know, Dallas." I tried to play it solemn, regretful even.

She saw right through that, rolling her eyes. "Stop acting like you give a fuck, Mr. Prescott."

I raised my brow. "We're not on first name basis anymore?"

"No." Tugging at her heavy coat, she rubbed her gloved hands together. "Why are you standing outside? It's cold as hell out here."

"It's January in Michigan," I said with a shrug. "And it's not that bad."

"The windchill is negative twenty," she deadpanned.

Across the street, I spotted my wife and her attorney. "And I'm willing to pay for your getaway if you get me out of this today."

Dallas Young was a monster in the courtroom, known for her ability to destroy her opponents with a smile on her beautiful face. Their firm specialized in family law, but she'd recently changed her focus to brokering marriages for business purposes and negotiating pre-nuptial agreements. Occasionally, she did favors and dipped her toes back into Divorce Court. I guess I was lucky that she liked me.

She shot me a sidelong glance. "Give me a few hours. I got you." Dallas pivoted on her heels, turning toward my soon-to-be-ex. Instead of greeting her, she spoke directly to her attorney. "John, you know this is a waste of time. Two days of marriage does not a divorce settlement make. Especially since your client misrepresented herself from the beginning. Lying about her age and pregnancy status sounds like fraud to me. Your bullshit filing doesn't change that."

My *darling* wife glared at me, her arms folded across her chest and her mouth pulled into a thin line. So fine, yet so ugly inside. And she hated my ass. Hell, I hated my ass, too. For falling for her lies.

Three days ago, I'd considered her a friend. Okay, so I considered her a business proposition. Her father owned one of the largest black-owned construction companies in Detroit. She wanted to stick it to her dad by marrying his biggest competition. *Me*. The "merger" was supposed to be beneficial for both of us. Until she turned psycho before I could get my dick wet. The fact that she'd concealed her pregnant belly didn't bother me as much as the fact that she'd managed to mask her deranged, delusional, damaged side.

"Cooper," Jacqueline snapped.

My gaze met hers.

Dallas stepped in front of me. "You don't get to talk to him. Tell it to the judge." She pulled my arm, prompting me to follow her into the building.

Hours later, my marriage was officially deemed invalid and I was on my second beer at the victory dinner. The judge had taken one look at Dallas' well-written response and granted an annulment without much fanfare, despite Jacqueline's dramatic hysterics in chambers.

"I thought she was going to beg the judge to make you stay married to her, Charming Bastard." Dallas took a sip of wine. "Even after you walked out on her the first night of your pseudo-honeymoon without a word or a goodbye, bitch."

I snorted. "It was actually over after the first hour, when I saw her very pregnant belly and asked her about it." Instead of owning up to her deception, Jacqueline went full-on fatal attraction. "The woman even threatened to kill the dog, after she locked herself in a closet, and after she demanded that I fuck her before I left."

Dallas choked. "Wait, she wanted to kill *her* dog?"

"Yeah, man." I winced. "I had to take it with me. Dropped it off at her sister's house."

Giggling, Dallas shook her head. "That heffa is nuts. Maybe you should have asked for a Temporary Restraining Order"

"Nah, I'm good. She's not *that* crazy."

"Well… You owe me. Big time."

"I got you," I said. She'd said the same thing to me earlier, and she'd meant every word. I did, too. "Thanks."

"It's what we do."

I glanced at my phone, at Grandad's text message again. Despite having plenty of time today, I still hadn't made any flight or rental car reservations. *I know I'm full of shit.*

"Coop?" Dallas arched a brow. "What's up? You look distracted."

Shrugging, I cleared my throat. "I have to go to Rosewood Heights."

She blinked. "Is it your grandfather?"

Dallas had proven herself to be a true confidante. I met Dallas years ago through her sister, Blake, who was close to an old *friend* of mine. Her ability to cut through bullshit impressed the hell out of me. I knew she was a keeper when she took all my damn money on the poker table *and* cussed my ass out for acting too cocky for my own good.

Through the years, I'd shared a lot of myself with her—opening up about my family, my past. She was easy to talk to. She'd never judged me and always told me the truth. She had the whole active listening thing down to a science. It was probably because she came from a family full of relationship therapists. Her parents were world-renowned marriage and family experts and many of her seven siblings had followed them into the field.

"Is he…?" She let the question hang in the air, signaling it was my turn to talk.

I shook my head. "No," I answered. "He asked for me."

"He called you?"

"He sent a text asking me to come home."

She sighed. "You have to go, Coop."

Meeting her concerned gaze, I said, "I know." The words *I'm scared* lodged in my throat. Because even if she knew it, I wasn't going to voice that out loud.

"So why are we here again?"

It was my idea to eat. Just another way of avoiding the

inevitable. I shrugged. "To eat," was my simple answer. "And to celebrate."

With narrowed eyes, she leaned forward. "Stop stalling, Coop."

I dropped my head. "I'm going."

When she squeezed my hand, I didn't pull away, needing the comfort she provided. "I would hate to see you miss out on seeing your grandfather one last time. Even if it's to tell him you love him."

I'd resolved myself to never seeing him again when I'd left the last time. We'd had a few short, but good conversations that felt final. His soft laughter still rang in my ears. I wanted to remember him laughing, not dying.

"He knows," I said.

"There's no harm in telling him again." She picked up her phone and busied herself doing something. A few minutes later, she held it up so I could see her screen. "Flight. Two hours. Get your ass to the airport." I gave her my credit card and she made the arrangements quickly. "All set." Instead of giving me back my card, she handed it to the server. "His treat."

Laughing, I said, "You're too comfortable with my money."

She grinned. "Your invoice will be in your inbox in the morning. I take tips." After I settled the bill, I walked her to her car. She gave me a quick hug and peered up at me. "Call me if you need me."

Nodding, I waited until she sunk into her car and took off before I jumped in my truck and headed to my place to pack a bag. It was a miracle that I'd made it to the airport on time, but I slid into my seat a few minutes before the door closed. The flight was relatively short, but felt too long because I couldn't concentrate on anything. Not my drink, not my work, and not the fine-ass flight attendant who'd slipped me her phone number with my peanuts. Somehow I knew that my life would be different tomorrow. And for the first time in years, I prayed that I would get there on time.

The halls of Rosewood Memorial Hospital were quiet. Visiting hours had ended an hour ago, but my last name guaranteed I had no problem going up to his room, especially since The Prescott Family was funding the new Cancer wing.

The room was empty, but I knew my parents and Ava were in the hospital somewhere. I stopped at the door and peered through the glass. The sight of him, so small, so still in the hospital bed gave me pause.

Opening the door, I approached him slowly. Gripping his hand, I squeezed. "Granddad?" I whispered.

He stirred a little, then his eyes opened quickly before they drifted closed again. Smiling, he said, "My main man," he said, his voice low, weak.

Tears burned my eyes. Swallowing rapidly, I croaked, "I'm here."

"Good. It's time."

Frowning, I leaned forward, "Old man, you better not die in front of me."

Even after I walked away from Rosewood Heights and our family company, Prescott Holdings, my relationship with the man in front of me had remained strong. The only thing he required of his family was honesty, which meant we had no choice but to tell it like it was. I'd never held back with him, and I wouldn't start today.

"Don't worry," he whispered. "I know who I'm talking to."

I let out a strained laugh. "Good to know."

Granddad opened his eyes again, this time they were

clear. Determined. "Glad you made it. I have something to tell you."

"What is it?"

"You did good, Cooper. I'm proud of you."

Shit. The damn tear fell before I could stop it.

"When I look at you, I see greatness." He squeezed my hand. "I love you, son."

Once again, words failed me. It seemed like I should say something profound, but the only thing that came out was, "I love you, too."

"Now, get out. Go get some sleep."

I did as I was told and checked myself into the room I'd reserved at Rosewood Inn. My phone buzzed before I could even take my boots off. And I knew who it was without even looking at the screen.

"Coop?" Ava's voice came through the receiver. "He's gone. Granddad died."

The Funeral

COOPER

That ass… Damn.

"Ouch." I winced when Ava smacked my back again. "What the…?"

My sister glared at me. "Can you be more obvious?"

I forced my attention away from the beauty that had captivated me from the moment she'd emerged from her car. Turning my gaze to my sister, I said, "Can you go somewhere else?" I pointed toward her husband and kids, standing near the door of the church. "Like over there with your family."

"You *are* my family."

"I meant the ones who listen to you and actually do what you tell them to do." I smirked. "Minding your business is full-time job, sis. You better get started."

Ava laughed. "Fool." She scanned the immediate area.

"This is hard. But I'm glad we don't have to do this alone, ya know?"

I hugged her. "Right."

We stood there for a few minutes, holding each other up. She pulled away, dabbing her eyes with a tissue. "I still can't believe he's really gone. I knew it was coming, but I didn't."

"I get it." Part of me always thought he'd be there. Living without him had never seemed like a viable option. "He wouldn't want us crying in public, though."

Ava snorted. "Never that. Prescotts don't cry. Ever."

"We keep it moving. Always."

That mantra had been on repeat in our home. Fall on the sidewalk and skin your knee? Take a deep breath and keep running. Sick? Take a nap, get up, and try again. Death? Do something to make them smile in the afterlife. Then, go to work. I'd learned that hard lesson when my Granny died and I tried to get out of a final exam. There was never an excuse to wallow.

Ava waved at Mother Parker as she shuffled toward the front of the church to take her seat. "I'm so happy you made it on time, Coop."

"Me, too."

The family hour was almost over, and the funeral would begin soon. After sitting in the sanctuary for fifteen minutes, staring at his body in that casket and watching the townspeople peer at him and then walk down the line greeting all of us, I couldn't take it anymore. It hadn't taken long for Ava to join me in the foyer.

"You good?" she asked.

Nodding, I explained again that I was as good as I promised to be. The days following Granddad's death were busy with work, solemn visitors, fried chicken, and countless errands for my mother. Ever the boss, Granddad had already planned his funeral down to the type of flowers, who could give remarks, and when to cut Bishop Roberts' eulogy off. My bossy little sister had already reminded the talkative reverend, letting him know in no uncertain terms, that twenty minutes was the limit.

My family had tithed in the Rosewood Heights Baptist Church for decades. The bishop knew the deal. One thing my grandfather hated was a long, drawn-out service. Two songs, a scripture, and a short message was all he'd required. It was why Granddad had made it a point to attend the early morning service, which was over within an hour in order to prepare for the much longer late morning service.

Ava squeezed my arm. "I need to check on the kids." She kissed my cheek. "Be right back."

The woman who'd haunted me for years was now hugging Ava on the other side of the room. As if I had no self-control, I found myself staring at that lovely ass again. *Damn*. She was beautiful. I watched as she tickled my niece and nephew, then hugged my oldest brother, Dominic. His big ass held on a little too long for my taste but that was my brother.

Moments later, she was standing in front of me, concern in her brown eyes and a sad smile on her full lips. "Hey," she breathed, before wrapping her arms around me in a tight hug.

She smelled like safety and felt like home. I knew I needed to pull away, but I couldn't bring myself to let her go. I'd done that once, which made me a damn fool. Because she'd walked away from my bullshit and fell in love. With someone else.

Burying my face in her neck, inhaling her sweet scent, I grumbled, "Good to see you, Ryleigh."

Slowly, she pulled away. "You, too."

I studied Ryleigh, took in her big brown eyes, her short hair, her thick curves in that tight skirt, and even her boots. Everything about her was better than the last time I'd seen her. She was radiant, glowing. The jealous part of me hated that it was most likely because she was happy without me.

Ryleigh was my sister's best friend, younger than me, but wise beyond her years. Although we'd grown up together, we'd really connected when I moved to Detroit after leaving the military. She was already established in the area, and she'd helped me find a place. Soon after, we were spending a lot of time together, eating dinner, and going to events in the city. Just hanging out. Before I knew it, I needed her.

Our relationship segued into lovers easily—*and secretly*. No one in my family knew that I'd fallen for Ryleigh Fields-now-Sullivan years ago and had never stopped loving her. The only person I'd ever told was Dallas—when it was over. And because I was a punk, despite our mutual connections, I hadn't seen Ryleigh in years. Not since my sister's wedding. She'd avoided me like the plague then, not that I blamed her. It felt damn good to lay eyes on her today, though, even if that was *all* I could lay on her.

Ryleigh squeezed my hand. "I'm so sorry. I know how much he meant to you."

I let out a haggard breath. "Thanks. I've missed you," I admitted softly, swiping my thumb over her hand. "I've thought about calling you."

"Honestly, I'm glad you didn't."

I smiled. She was always brutally honest. I loved that about her. "That's fair."

Things hadn't ended well with us, especially since they didn't *really* end in the way a relationship between adults should end. Back then, I was about my money and proving to my father that I could make it without Prescott Holdings. I'd never expected to fall in love.

True to form, though, my sabotage game was in full effect and I'd fucked up. I hadn't shown up for something really important to her. Then, I didn't show the next day. And the next day. Until I knew there was no turning back.

"How's your husband? What's his name again?" I asked, unable to turn off my inner asshole.

"*Martin*. And he's perfect. He had a family funeral."

"Sorry," I told her. "I heard you had a baby." The smile she blessed me with in that moment made me want to pull a "*baby, please*" moment like the one she loved so much from her favorite show, *A Different World*. "You'll have to show me a pic."

Beaming, she said, "Maybe later."

Dallas stepped over to us, bumping Ryleigh's hip. "He's adorable. My little Chunk Chunk."

Ryleigh had introduced me to Dallas and her large clan years ago. For the first few months after I'd ghosted her, I had also made the decision to stop hanging with the Youngs. But Dallas nipped that shit in the bud one night when she'd called me on my *obvious* feelings for Ryleigh and my fucked up way of dealing with them. That had been the actual turning point in our friendship, and it was the moment I'd confessed everything to her.

"Stop drooling," Dallas muttered, pulling me into a hug. "You're about five years too late for a second chance."

"Shut up," I grumbled. "But thanks for coming."

Dallas eyed me. "Of course."

Ryleigh gestured toward the sanctuary. "I'm going to catch up with the girls." When she tried to walk away, I gripped her wrist, halting her retreat. Pausing, she sighed. "Coop."

"I have so much I want to say to you."

"It's okay," she whispered.

"It's not okay," I argued.

She pulled her hand from my grasp. "Seriously. It is."

Keeping my voice low, I said, "I… I'm sorry."

Her shoulders fell. Then, she met my waiting gaze. "Things turned out the way they were supposed to turn out. I'm happy, and I'm *happily* married. Take care, Coop."

Then, she walked away without a backward glance.

To my right, Dallas approached me again. "She's happy, Cooper. Let it go. Sometimes we fu—" She cleared her throat and scanned the area, most likely remembering she was in a church. "Mess… up. We learn and we don't do it again. Right?" She tugged on my hand. "Want me to sit with you?" She held up a box of Kleenex. "I can be your tissue assistant."

I wrapped my arm around her shoulder. "I can handle my own tissue." Sighing, I added, "Besides, I have to sit with my family. But thanks."

"We'll drink all the cognac tonight," she whispered.

"Promise?"

She nodded. "Definitely." Putting her hands together, she peered up at the ceiling. "Forgive me, Lord."

"IS THERE a reason why we have to do this today?" I tugged at my tie and set a plate of Mom's sweet potatoes and collard greens on the end table. "I couldn't even finish Mama Lil's pot roast. That shit was good as hell."

Granddad had requested the reading of the will to be directly following the repast. All of us were present and accounted for in the formal living room of Prescott Manor, my family's home.

Hunter glanced at his watch. "What time is the attorney arriving?"

My twin had been through a lot over the past year, dealing with an illness that had wrecked his life. As a result, he'd retreated to the west coast and hid it from the rest of the family. He hadn't even told me until two months ago. Sworn to secrecy, I had no choice but to honor his wish to stay silent. But that shit was hard, especially since I knew he'd needed the support. Seeing him today was good, though. Hunter had lost a lot weight and used a cane, but the fact that he *could* walk made me feel confident he would beat it.

"He's already here, son," Mama said. "Your father is handling some Prescott business with him. They'll be in shortly."

Suddenly, I had no appetite for the food next to me. Annoyed at my father's refusal to stop doing "Prescott business" for one day, I shot Dominic a glare. "Because he can't not work for a day," I mumbled. "Not even on the day he buried his father."

Needless to say, my father and I didn't get along. We hadn't seen eye to eye since we'd agreed that football wasn't my sport in fifth grade. From the time I was old enough to write, he'd told anyone who would listen that I would take over as CEO of the company one day. Which meant I couldn't do anything other than live, breathe, and sleep Prescott Holdings. Of course, that didn't work for me. And I'd rebelled swiftly and disrespectfully as often as I could. The strain in our relationship still hadn't recovered.

"Cooper." My mother's warning voice effectively shut my ass up. "Don't."

Without another word, I poured a full glass of water and took a long gulp, slamming it onto the table.

Dom shot me a sideways glance. "Really? What the hell are you? Two?"

I smirked, shoving him playfully. "Shut up."

My father entered the room with the attorney right behind him a short while later. They spent several minutes explaining the procedure for the will reading. Granddad had videotaped his wishes and when his face appeared on the big screen television that had been moved into the room for the occasion, I swallowed past the lump that had formed in my throat.

Granddad had obviously thought of everything. In the recording, he was strong. His voice was solid and assured. As always, he stayed on task, rolling out his wishes to us in age order.

After Dominic's turn, I was up.

"Cooper?" Granddad said, his eyes locked on the camera. "It's time for you to come home and take your rightful place at Prescott Holdings."

"I'm not moving back to damn Rosewood Heights," I muttered under my breath.

"And before you say you're not moving back to damn Rosewood Heights," Granddad continued, shocking the hell out of me, "I've seen the strides you've made away from us. You've built your own empire, which is tremendous *and* expected. No one ever assumed you wouldn't. Remember that."

I tried not to let any tears fall. I failed. Because even if Granddad knew I would succeed, my father sure as hell didn't. And he'd made that clear on more than one occasion.

"But…" Granddad coughed. "You. Can. Do. Both. The company needs you. Your family needs you. It's time."

Over the next few minutes, Granddad read through a small list of possessions that he wanted me to have, including the gold ring my great grandfather had left him. I remembered the first time I'd seen it. Right then, I'd declared that I was going to have a ring like that one day. I couldn't have been more than six-years-old. Granddad had promised me then that I would have it one day. And he'd kept that promise by leaving me *his* ring.

I cleared my throat and sucked in a deep breath as fresh tears threatened to fall. Although Granddad's death wasn't unexpected, I still couldn't believe he wasn't a phone call away anymore, that he wouldn't be available to provide his own brand of wisdom when I needed it.

After he'd addressed everyone in the room, the video ended. From that point on, the attorney handled the money, the property, and everything else not covered in the video. And all I could think about was Granddad. I didn't need the money; I didn't even want it. I just wanted more time to learn from him, to talk to him. I needed to tell him face-to-face that I couldn't do it. I'd always done what he'd asked, but I couldn't—*and wouldn't*—move back to Rosewood Heights.

After the lawyer left, my father stood. "I also have something for you all." He pulled out several white envelopes. "Your grandfather wrote you each a personal letter with strict instructions that you read them and do as he requested. Your inheritance is not contingent on this, but these are his final wishes." For a minute, I thought my father was on the verge of tears. But he simply took in a deep breath and handed each of us an envelope.

Instead of opening them right away, we all stared at each other. Eventually, Ava broke the ice first, opening her letter and reading silently. When I opened my envelope, a cashier's check fell out. It was payable to me, with "for a special project" written on the memo line. I glanced at my siblings, who were each immersed in their own letters. Slowly, I unfolded the piece of paper.

Cooper,

Since you like to keep things short and sweet, this letter won't be too long.

Life is about more than winning. Stop trying to prove something to your father that he already knows. Perhaps if you just talked to him, you would know it, too. Get your shit together and stop holding grudges that don't matter. Someone has to make the first move. It's time.

I have a special request of you. One that you're uniquely qualified for. There's a woman, Louise Fox. She's very important to me and I let her down a long time ago. She once lived at the end of Prospect Cove, in the Tudor style home on the corner. The house is in bad shape. Although she still owns it, she hasn't resided there for a long while. I made a promise to her the last time we spoke that I would have her home restored to its former glory. Please see to it that it's done. It will make her smile.

I love you.

Granddad

P.S. Shit happens in life that you can't change. We make mistakes that have lasting effects. Sometimes time doesn't heal all wounds. But never let that stop you from striving to do better.

I read the letter three more times before I tore my gaze from Granddad's distinctive script. I'd already resigned myself into ignoring his request to move back home, but I wouldn't let him down on this. If he wanted Ms. Fox's home restored, that was exactly what I would do.

Chapter 1

ANGEL

"This place is a dump."

A laugh I shouldn't have let escape did. "Mehki!" I sent my son a mock glare. "That's not nice."

My six-year-old glanced around the foyer of the large house. He pushed his glasses up on his face. "You told me never to lie."

I rubbed his hair. "That doesn't mean you have to say everything that comes to mind either. What if Aunt Lou was here?"

He frowned as if confused by my question. "But she died. Why would she be here?"

A pang of sadness washed over me. My great-aunt Louise had put everything she had into this home, until she couldn't anymore. I scanned the immediate area, trying to figure out a plan of action.

Mehki's soft hand slipped into mine. "Are you sad, Mommie?"

The tears that had been just near the surface all day spilled down my cheeks. I nodded. "Yes, babe."

The news that my aunt had passed away had hit me like a brick. Because I'd always planned to visit, I'd always wanted to spend more time, I'd always wanted to learn how to make her famous cheesecake or her delicious pepper steak. I just never made the time. Between work, Mehki, and life I always had something else to do.

Guilt washed over me as I recalled the last time I'd spoken with Aunt Lou on the phone. She'd asked me to come to Rosewood Heights to go over her end of life business and I told her I'd be here soon. That was three months ago. Now, she was dead.

I felt my baby's little arms wrap around me and I hugged him back. "I'll be okay, though." I kissed the top of his head. "We got this."

"We got this," he mimicked, squeezing my waist. "Mommie?"

Pulling back, I brushed my thumbs over his cheeks. "Yes?"

"I think Aunt Lou knew you loved her."

I smiled. "Why do you say that?"

"Because you told her every time you talked to her on the phone. I heard it."

My heartbeat pounded in my ears. "Thanks, babe. You made Mommie feel better."

Sort of. The last time I'd spoken with Aunt Lou we'd had a really good conversation, about regrets and life choices. She'd urged me to get some happiness—and a man—while I was still young enough to enjoy it. I'd argued that I was too busy to wade into a dating pool full of men I didn't know—or *want* to know. My chance at love died before Mehki was born.

Another pang of sadness welled up in me. One thing Aunt Lou was right about was the effect of regret on a life. It had the power to propel things forward or stop everything in its track. It was a savage emotion, able to trip me up in two-point-two seconds.

"I'm hungry." Mehki pulled out his tablet. "What's that smell?"

"Moth balls," I muttered, scowling at the stale smell flowing through the house. "We should open up the windows." I walked into the living room and cracked open a window. The mild breeze floated into the room and I inhaled deeply. "This is better."

I busied myself opening more windows in the dining room, the sunroom, and the kitchen. Once I made it back into the living room, I placed my hands on my hips and sighed. The five-bedroom house hadn't been lived in for a while. It wasn't as bad as it could've been, but it wasn't that great either. There was obvious damage on the roof, a clicking sound coming from the vents, and I had a feeling there were other hidden problems that would cost a fortune to fix. Such a shame, though. The huge home was once a focal point in the community. Aunt Lou loved to tell me all about the annual garden parties she used to throw and the Rosewood Heights Women's Association Tea she hosted every month.

As if he'd read my thoughts, Mehki said, "We can't sleep here, Mommie. It's dirty."

Once again, I couldn't help the laugh that burst through. "That's why we're here. To clean up." Yet, as I glanced around once more, I prayed that no one wanted to visit the house. Mehki was right, it really wasn't suitable for guests.

Aunt Lou had only passed away yesterday, but there was so much to do before my parents arrived tomorrow. She didn't want a funeral, but she'd requested that we commemorate her life with a short ceremony at the beach before we released her ashes in the ocean.

As the executor of her estate, I was in charge of getting everything ready. I hadn't had a chance to read through everything she'd left for me to decipher. And even if I had, law wasn't my strong suit. I preferred spreadsheets, cost analysis, budgets, and forecasts. But I would handle business as best as I could.

First things first… I dialed Aunt Lou's attorney and informed him that I'd made it to town. He'd agreed to meet us at the house within an hour, which meant we had to make the best of it until we could head back to the inn, where I'd booked a room.

"Let's order pizza," I suggested.

Mehki groaned. "Do we have to? I hate pizza."

"You just ate pizza last week?"

"Well, I don't like it anymore."

I picked a piece of lint off of my sweater. "I don't believe you."

"Can we have a real dinner?" He glanced up at me. "I would like chicken and rice."

My shoulders fell. "Mehki, I can't cook here."

My son was spoiled. He hated eating out. What six-year old hated McDonalds? Mehki Landon Crawford, that's who. "How about Wendy's? You can get chicken nuggets."

He made a disgusted face. "We had Wendy's on the way here."

Shit, he's right. I'd stopped at the restaurant right before we hit the road for the hours-long drive here from Charleston. "Jimmy Johns?" I asked, desperate for a solution that didn't involve a trip to the grocery store.

Mehki let out an exaggerated groan. "No."

"Krispy Kreme?" Donuts for dinner sounded good. I was due for a cheat day.

Shaking his head rapidly, he said, "Mommie?"

Oh Lord. When he said my name in that high-pitched voice and looked at me with those puppy dog eyes, I was toast. "Yes?"

"How about we have tomato soup and grilled cheese sandwiches?"

His favorite. And it still involved a trip to the grocery store. "How about we have that for lunch tomorrow after I've had time to go to the store. For now, let's pick something quick. If you don't pick, I will."

He hummed, tapping his little chin with his finger. "Orange chicken and rice."

"Great," I chirped. "Panda Express is down the street. We can walk there and grab dinner."

"I'm thirsty."

I dug into my bag and pulled out a bottle of water, handing it to him. "Drink this. I'm going to head into the kitchen and get started."

"And I'm going to play this game," he announced, turning his attention back to his tablet.

Good. I grabbed the bag full of cleaning supplies I'd brought with me and walked into the kitchen. Spinning around, I took in all of the cabinet space, the wallpaper, the older appliances, and the table by the large window where Aunt Lou used to read the newspaper. It looked just like I remembered. Yellow walls, hardwood floors, frilly curtains. Aunt Lou sure hated modern décor. Her room was probably still pink and lacy. I made a mental note to call Tierra, my best friend. She was an interior designer and a realtor in Charleston. I definitely needed her guidance if I was going to put the house on the market.

Aside from the dust, the kitchen was pretty neat. No dirty dishes in the sink, nothing out of place. I knew Aunt Lou once had a housekeeper, but it was obvious the woman hadn't been there in a long time. Maybe she grew tired of paying for the service? Shrugging, I opened cabinets, mentally taking inventory of what was there. Luckily, the refrigerator was empty save for a few water bottles and bottle of salad dressing. The dishwasher only had one glass inside. Once I was satisfied that nothing nasty would jump out at me, I pulled out bowls for the Clorox and the Pine Sol. Disinfecting surfaces was first up.

After realizing I'd forgotten the cleaning rags I'd purchased, I pulled out several drawers and eventually located a few clean dish towels. "Yes!" I cheered. To myself. Because no one was there. "Now, if I could snap my fingers and everything would be done. I wonder if I… And apparently, I love talking to the air."

Laughing at myself, I turned the faucet. Nothing. I twisted the other knob. Nothing. I bent to open the cabinet under the sink, like I actually knew what I was doing. I noticed a jar with a wrench and some other tool inside. Standing, I tried again. This time, everything came out.

"Oh shit!" I shouted.

Water sprayed everywhere—on the window, on the floor, in my face, on my brand knew sweater, in my hair. It was no longer a faucet; it was a fountain. *Damnit.* My wash-and-go was definitely ruined because I was soaked.

"Shit! Shit! Shit!" I probably said that word fifty times in under one minute, each in a different tone and decibel. After several tries with my slippery hands, I turned the water off.

"Mommie?"

I jumped, holding my chest. "You scared me."

"You cussed. You told me that shit was a bad word." I rushed over to him and clasped my hand over his mouth. He cringed, backing away from me. He wiped his mouth. "Yuck! You got me wet, Mommie."

"Shut it," I ordered. "Go sit down in the living room and play your game."

He pointed and jumped back. "Ugh, why was the water brown?"

"Because this day sucks," I answered. "And now I need to call a fuckin' plumber," I added under my breath. Sighing, I wiped my forehead. "Shi—" I glanced back at him. "Shoot. Mehki, open that drawer and grab me a towel."

He did as I asked and ran over to me, handing me the towel. I shook it out and screamed when a spider fell onto the floor. It wasn't dead either. It was ugly, nasty, and *about* to be dead, though. I lifted my foot, prepared to kill that thing when Mehki screamed.

"What?" I asked, confused.

"Don't kill it," he yelled. "We need spiders in the world. They are good for the environment."

Having a high IQ kid with an eidetic memory who devoured every book he could, even at his age, sometimes made parenting harder than it should be. Mehki was gifted, skipping first grade without any effort. Some of his teachers had already insisted he was a child prodigy.

I didn't take my eye off of the spider, which had stopped moving. It was watching me, waiting to jump on my ass at any moment.

"Mehki, get it out of here then."

My super-son snatched the towel from me and scooped up the spider with it. "I want to study it."

"No. Toss it outside so it can help the environment."

He bolted from the kitchen and I stared at the ceiling.

Counting to ten, I walked back to the sink. *Guess I better call somebody.*

"Mommie!"

I rushed toward the front of the house, slowing when I saw Mehki standing at the door talking to a man. A *fine* ass man. My gaze dropped to my wet clothes and my fingers instinctively touched my drenched hair. *And I probably look like a wet mop.*

I wiped my hands on my jeans and stepped up the door. "Hi. Can I help you?"

The man, dressed in dark jeans and a fitted long-sleeved shirt, grinned. "Hi, I'm—"

"Are you here to fix the sink?" Mehki asked.

"Um…" The man scratched the back of his neck. "No."

"Okay." Mehki slammed the door.

"Mehki!" I shouted, opening the door again. "I'm so sorry."

But the man didn't look angry, he looked… amused. The smile on his face widened. "It's okay. My kind of guy. He's obviously very protective of his… *momma*?" The question hung in the air. Cute Stranger was fishing to see if I was the mother. A lot of interested men did that. Many of them turned the other way when I told them the truth.

I nodded. "Yeah… I'm the momma and he is very protective."

"Cooper Prescott." He held out his hand.

I started to slip my hand in his, but remembered my hand was likely clammy from all that rusty water. "I would shake your hand, but I had a mishap with the faucet in the kitchen. Angel Crawford." Frowning, I struggled to remember where I'd heard the Prescott name before. Then, it dawned on me. "Prescott?"

"Yes."

Rosewood Heights could have probably been named Prescott Heights. The family was well known, well-established in the small town. Aunt Lou never seemed to care much about them, though. She often had a sneer on her face when she referred to the senior Prescott, the one she'd grown up with.

I leaned against the door. "What can I do for you?" I glanced down at Mehki, who was silently watching Cutie Prescott. *I mean…* Cooper Prescott.

"Is Ms. Fox home?" Cooper asked.

The familiar sadness crept over me again. "Unfortunately, no. She passed away."

He blinked, obviously surprised by the news. "Wow. I'm sorry for your loss." Averting his gaze, he mumbled something to himself before meeting my eyes again. "I came over because my grandfather asked me to handle something for Ms. Fox."

Curious, I said, "I wasn't aware that my aunt talked to your grandfather."

Shrugging, he said, "Honestly, I didn't know either. Do you mind if I come in?"

"Oh." I nodded and stepped aside. "Sure." He stepped over the threshold into the foyer. And, *damn*, he was tall. And solid. And he smelled good. I hurried to the living room and pretended to straighten up, with Mehki on my heels. "Sit down, baby," I told my protector. Turning to Cooper, I gestured toward the large sofa. "Have a seat." I sat on the smaller sofa. Once again, Mehki was right next to me.

"When did Ms. Fox die?" Cooper asked.

"Yesterday," I replied. "She went peacefully."

"I'm sorry for your loss," he repeated. "My grandfather died very recently, too."

"Oh, I didn't know that. I'm sorry."

"Are you from Rosewood Heights?"

I shook my head. "No, I live in Charleston. I'm just here to get everything ready for Aunt Lou's…" I rubbed my ear. "…her memorial. I'm also the executor of her estate so I have to take care of her business."

"Okay, so you *are* the person I need to talk to then?"

"Why would you need to talk *me*? If this is about money she owed your family, I'm going to have to—"

"My grandfather requested that I restore," he glanced around the room, "this house."

"What?" I stood and paced the room. "Why would *your* grandfather ask *you* to restore *this* house for *my* Aunt Lou?"

Cooper stood, too. "I don't know." He hunched one shoulder. "But it was one of his final wishes."

I stared at the far wall. The painting currently hanging there had always been there. It was of Aunt Lou in a field of grass. I loved the portrait because she was smiling, carefree. There was a light in her eyes, one that I had never seen up close. Ever. I'd often imagined that the painting was commissioned by a man—someone who'd made her happy once, someone who'd made her feel loved.

Aunt Lou had married twice, but never had children of her own. Her first husband died before I was born and she divorced her second husband right before she turned sixty. She'd confessed to me that she hadn't wanted to go into her twilight years tethered to "that old fool". In hindsight, I didn't think she'd loved either of those men.

Although she was a loner, she'd often had us visit for a few weeks in the summer. I always had a good time with her. We'd developed a special bond, one that she didn't have with my mother. Aunt Lou had been there for every big event of my life—recitals, sports tournaments, graduations, and my wedding. And she'd dropped everything to come stay with me after my husband's death, to help with Mehki.

"Mrs. Crawford?"

I blinked, shaking myself from my thoughts. "I'm sorry. You were saying something?"

"Maybe I should come back tomorrow? You obviously have a lot you're dealing with. We can talk about this another time."

He was right. I needed to investigate. I needed time to figure out what all of this meant. There was obviously a story here, but I had no clue where to start. "Good idea," I agreed. "I have a lot to get done around here before tomorrow. And my son is hungry."

"Very hungry," Mehki corrected.

I smiled. "Got it."

Mehki approached Cooper. "Sir?"

Cooper looked down at my son. "Yes?"

"Can you fix a sink?" Mehki asked. "Water sprayed everywhere and Mommie cussed a lot when she got wet. We *have* to clean up a little around here before we can leave. It's important."

Cutie Prescott met my gaze and grinned. "I think I can help with that."

"Really?" I asked. "Well, I won't stop you."

He followed Mehki and me into the kitchen, and it didn't take long for him to get to work. Half an hour later, he'd fix the faucet using tools he just so happened to have in his car. When he was finished, he tested it out by washing his hands.

I handed him the last towel. *Now, I need to go to Target to get more supplies.* "Here you go. No paper towels or napkins."

His eyes locked on mine as he dried his hands. "No need."

Tucking a strand of hair behind my ear, I said, "Thanks for your help, Mr. Prescott."

"Cooper," he insisted. "And you're welcome, Angel."

Lawd... The way my name rolled off his tongue seemed to increase the temperature in the room—and my body. *I need to get myself together.* I wasn't a corny teenager or even a desperate woman. *Why is this man pushing all my buttons?* "Who said you could call me by my first name?" I asked, attempting to take back some of my control.

He laughed. "Ah, you got me. I guess you didn't give me permission."

Cracking up, I waved him off. "I'm just playin'. Thanks for everything. And I definitely want to talk about this house thing when things die down."

"Sounds like a plan." He pulled out a business card and handed it to me. "Call my cell."

I studied the card. Another checkmark in the 'I'm intrigued' column for Cooper. I'd always liked men who worked with their hands. "You work in construction?"

"I do."

Arching a brow, I asked, "In Detroit?"

"Yes, ma'am." He flashed a dimpled smile. "In the D."

Cutie Prescott was a charming muthafucka. And I caught that emphasis on *the D*. It made me think about another *D*. Under his pants.

"*Angel, get your shit together.*"

"Excuse me?"

Shit, I said that out loud. "Nothing," I lied, grabbing Mehki's hand and starting toward the front door. "I'll give you a call soon."

He brushed by me, leaving me with the consolation prize of another whiff of his cologne. "Good. I'll be in town for another week or so."

"Alright."

He walked outside of the house and turned back to me. Dropping his gaze to Mehki, he said, "I saw you let that spider go when I got here."

"I didn't want Mommie to kill it," Mehki said.

"I used to collect them."

My son's eyes lit up. "Really? I want a Chilean Rose tarantula, but Mommie said no."

Cooper looked at me. "Do it. They're fun pets."

I grimaced. "Not in this life. He can visit them in a museum or a zoo or something."

"I'll work on her," Cooper told Mehki with a wink.

"Thank you!" Mehki grinned. "Can you come back tomorrow?"

Laughing, Cooper said, "Not tomorrow. But I'll see you again." He held up a hand and Mehki slapped him a high five. "Bye, Angel Crawford."

My stomach turned. "Bye, Cooper Prescott."

Then, he was gone. And I was… still intrigued. *Charming muthafucka.*

Chapter 2

COOPER

"You're still here, bruh?"

Dominic greeted the hostess at the door and made his way over to my booth, greeting every regular in the place before he slid in across from me.

"Took you long enough." I sipped my hot coffee. "I ordered without you."

My brother made no move to pick up the menu, because we'd eaten at The Little Rose for years. Mama Lil's blueberry pancakes were a gift from heaven. And Mama Lil was, too. The older woman had saved my ass from myself and bad consequences more times than not over the years, back when my agenda was to piss my father off by any means necessary. Each time I found myself nursing a hangover or hiding from the world, she would open her door to me and give me sage advice.

Dominic scanned the restaurant. "Mama Lil here? I

don't trust that new cook she hired. He messed up my omelet last time."

"I don't know." Without looking, I pointed toward the waitress taking an order from the couple at the table next to ours. "She took my order."

"You mean the woman staring at yo' ass?"

I didn't bother to look, but I knew Dominic was right. The young waitress had definitely flirted her way through my order. I had to correct her three damn times and make her repeat it after me to be sure she got it right. "If you say so."

The waitress made her way back over to us and poured Dom a cup of coffee. "What would you like to eat?" she asked my brother.

Dom placed his order. "Is Mama Lil in the building?"

"I don't know," she answered.

I glanced up at her and smiled. "Can you go check, sweetheart?"

The waitress grinned, tucking a strand of hair behind her ear. "Sure. I'll check."

Winking, I thanked her. When she walked away, I looked over at Dom, who was shaking his head. "What?" I asked with a shrug.

He poured cream into his mug. "You don't even realize you're doing that shit, do you?"

Feigning confusion, I repeated, "What?"

He waved a dismissive hand my way. "Nothing."

Hey, I'm a flirt. I knew what the hell I was doing. And it worked. "It's a gift, man. I can't turn it off." I laughed. "I bet you my food will be free."

"If your food is free, you can pay my bill."

"Done," I agreed.

Dom leaned back in his seat and eyed me skeptically. "You never answered my question, though."

I frowned. "What question?"

"You still here? I thought for sure you'd be back in Detroit right now, avoiding your family responsibilities."

I mulled over my brother's words, torn between a version of the truth or the whole truth. Dom was close to all of us, taking his oldest brother duties seriously. He never expected us to be anything other than ourselves. Even though he didn't agree with my choice to leave Rosewood Heights and the family business behind, he'd never tried to change my mind. He'd only ever supported me. We had an understanding, and I knew that I could count on him to have my back at all times.

"Well?" Dom prodded. "Are you going to talk?"

"I missed my flight," I lied. I'd actually willingly canceled my flight. But I wasn't going to tell him that. "So I figured I should at least make some plans to do what Granddad asked." That was the truth. Maybe not the whole truth, though.

"You know I don't buy that shit. What's up, bruh?"

"Granddad asked me to restore an old house in town," I admitted.

"He also asked you to come home and take your place in the business," Dom added. "Don't forget that part."

Forgetting *that* part wasn't an option. Because every time I closed my eyes, I saw Granddad on that damn video asking me to run the company that he'd devoted his life to. And every time I opened my eyes, I knew I'd be the man who wouldn't honor my grandfather's wish.

"You know that's not going to happen," I said, my voice low. I twirled the mug, avoiding eye contact with my very intuitive and somewhat annoying big brother.

There was a part of me that felt ashamed to admit that out loud. Because my grandfather had never broken a promise to me, and I was intent on ignoring one of his final requests. The will reading had put everything in perspective for me. That last text, my last conversation with him… the entire time he was telling me to come *home*. Not just for a visit, but for a life. The only problem was I already had a life—in Detroit. I already had a business—in Detroit. I had no plans to leave all of that behind to be stuck behind a desk, working with my father day in and day out.

"Why?" Dom asked.

"I can't just move," I told him. "I have obligations, I have…" I couldn't even finish the sentence because I didn't really have anything *other* than my business holding me there. Yes, I had friends, a network… But those people would be there whether I stayed in Detroit or not. And, honestly, my business would run smoothly no matter where I lived. Yet, trading my freedom for the chokehold of tradition and duty didn't feel right to me. It never had. "Shit, I just don't want to do it."

"I get it," Dom said.

I studied my brother. I knew it was hard on him, always being there, always being the steady son and brother. I wondered if he was ready for something new.

"In the end, though, they're just excuses," Dom continued. "You've always done what *you* wanted to do. But sometimes you have to do things you don't want to do, bruh. Dad is getting older. He wants to retire soon, spend more time with Mom."

The thought of my father retiring had never even crossed my mind. "Has he mentioned that to you?"

"He didn't have to, man. He's tired. And Mom is tired of him. I see the struggle. I hear about the canceled dinners and the postponed vacations."

"Well, I don't want to have to cancel dinners and postpone vacations either. Prescott Holdings is not my endgame. I don't want to live my life like Dad *and* Granddad lived theirs, working long hours inside, going to board meetings, brokering deals."

Dom raised a brow. "Isn't that what you do now for your business?"

Well, shit. Of course, that was what I did now. It was what every business owner did to ensure their business was successful.

"Listen, we're all here to support you," he explained. "You're not alone. You never were."

I felt alone, though. Closing my eyes, I let out a harsh breath. "Just drop it. My life is in Michigan, not Rosewood Heights."

"Why not just think about it? Give it some time, visit the office." Dom shrugged. "Maybe nothing is like you think it will be."

"Bruh…"

"Seriously, Coop. You—"

"Oh my goodness!"

I looked over to my right and grinned at the sight of Mama Lil shuffling toward our table. I stood. "Mama Lil." I hugged her tightly.

She patted my back. "Good to see you again, CooCoo."

I rolled my eyes. "Mama Lil," I groaned, annoyed at the nickname I couldn't seem to escape, no matter how old I was. "You promised."

Pulling back, she laughed waving her dish towel at me. "I know, I know. But I can't help it. I still remember you going crazy over that chocolate cereal. Shoot, I had to keep a box here in the restaurant for you."

"Tell me about it," Dom muttered. "He probably still eats it."

I glared at my brother. "No."

"Aw, boy, stop." Mama Lil patted my cheek. "It's okay if you still love Cocoa Puffs. No judgement. You'll always be my CooCoo." She cracked up.

Dominic laughed, too. "Hey, Mama Lil." He hugged her. "I'm glad you're here."

"Don't worry," she assured them. "I put my special touch on both of your meals. They'll be out shortly. I just wanted to come see y'all before I left."

"You're leaving already?" I asked.

She shrugged. "Yeah. That Ry-Girl is on me to slow down."

I caught Dom staring at me when Mama Lil mentioned Ryleigh. *Did he know something*?

"It's probably for good reasons," Dom said. "You've been working a long time. It's time for you to enjoy life."

"Oh, I still have fun," she insisted. "I got my friends. We play cards, go to the casino… I also spend a lot of time with Ryleigh and Martin in Michigan." She pinned me with one of her infamous don't-try-me glances. "How come I never see you?"

"You're always too busy for me," I said.

"Yeah, right. I'm old but I'm not stupid. I know you try to stay far away from Ryleigh, boy. That worst-kept secret is out."

Dom barked out a laugh. "I'm glad someone told him the truth. He thought he was slick, Mama Lil." He gave her a high five. "So smart, yet so slow."

I glanced at Mama Lil, then at Dom. "So everybody knows about me and Ryleigh?"

"Boy, please." She stepped aside when the waitress brought the food out and set it in front of us. "I don't know *everybody* is, but I been knew. I saw you at Ava's wedding, chile. Staring at Ry-Girl with those sad eyes."

"Looking pitiful," Dom cosigned. "Sad and pitiful."

"What the …?" I shifted in my seat. "Why didn't you tell me you knew?"

Dom hunched his left shoulder, biting into a piece of bacon. "I figured you'd tell me when you were ready."

"You never could hide anything from me," Mama Lil said. "But it was a good thing you acted a complete, pitiful fool at that wedding. 'Cause if you had come to your senses, Ryleigh might not have let Martin love her. And he *does* love her."

I love her, too. "I'm glad she's happy." The words tasted sour and disingenuous. But what the hell else could I say? "She deserves it."

"Definitely," Dom agreed. "Married life looks good on her. Right, Coop?"

I glared at my brother. "Yes," I said, thought clenched teeth.

"It's okay to be jealous." Mama Lil squeezed my cheek, much like she used to when I was younger. "You messed up, but it's okay. We live and learn."

The last thing I wanted to hear—again—was that. Even if it was the truth. "These pancakes look good," I said, moving the subject away from Ryleigh. "Thanks for hooking me up with the extra blueberries." Which I'd only started eating *because* it was Ryleigh's favorite.

"How long will you be in town, son?" she asked.

"Another week or so." *Maybe longer*. For some reason, I kept extending my departure date. I told myself it was because of the Fox house, but there was more to it. Something was preventing me from hopping on the next flight out of here.

The bell above the door rang and Angel walked into the dinner with two older people, another woman, and her son. The little boy pointed at me and sprinted toward my booth.

"Hi, Mr. Cooper!" He waved.

"Well, who is this?" Mama Lil asked.

"I'm Mehki," the boy announced, before he told me, "We saw another spider in the house. I think there's a family."

"Really?" I said, staring at Angel as she approached the table. I didn't even bother to hide my perusal, letting my gaze travel from her shoes to her hips to the cleavage just barely peeking out of her blouse to the gold necklace she wore around her neck to her mouth… *Damn, that mouth.* It tripped me up the first time I'd seen her. And those light brown eyes. She was beautiful—soaking wet *and* dressed to impress. "I hear you have another little friend?"

Angel rolled her eyes. "Don't remind me. They're everywhere."

"Ah, I see."

"You should come over," Mehki suggested. "Maybe we can catch some."

Pulling Mehki closer to her, Angel said, "How about we do not disturb them if we don't have to, babe?" Peering down at me, she said, "I'm sorry. He's been talking about you for the last two days. He was super excited when we saw you through the window."

I held her gaze as I sipped my coffee. "It's no problem."

"I'm sure you're in the middle of something." She gripped her throat, drawing my attention from her eyes to her neck. "We won't bother you anymore."

"You're not bothering me," I told her before I introduced them to Dom and Mama Lil. "Do you like pancakes, Mehki?"

The boy nodded rapidly. "With lots of butter and syrup. Mommie makes the best."

"Really?" I couldn't take my eyes off of her. "Mommie cooks?"

Mehki shouted yes. "She's the best!"

The more I learned about Angel, the more I wanted to learn. "Maybe your Mommie can make me some pancakes when I come over to help you find all the spiders?"

The corner of Angel's mouth lifted. "Will you be ridding the house of those spiders?" she asked. "If so, you can have all the pancakes you like."

I raised a brow. "Promise?"

She let out a shaky breath. "Deal. I wanted to talk to you about the house anyway. I decided to stay in Rosewood Heights a little longer, because I want to be able to settle Aunt Lou's affairs."

"Oh," Mama Lil's hand flew to her mouth. "You're *Lou's* niece, Angel?"

Angel nodded. "Yes, ma'am."

"I haven't seen you since you were a little girl." Mama Lil hugged her. "I'm so sorry for your loss, baby. Your aunt was a force to be reckoned with in this town. She talked about you a lot, told me all about you and your baby. She was so proud. We were good friends, ya know?"

"I'm so glad to hear that." Angel flashed a wobbly smile. She pointed toward the window. "My mother is here, too."

"I remember Theresa," Mama Lil said. "I'll have to go over and say hi."

"We released her ashes into the ocean," Mehki announced proudly. "I did the honors."

Angel shrugged nervously, guilt passing over her face. "I'm sorry. She didn't want it to be public."

"I know, sweetie." Mama Lil grabbed Angel's hand. "I spoke with Lou about her plans a few months ago."

"If you don't mind," Angel shifted her purse to her

other arm, "I'd love to ask you some questions about Aunt Lou sometime soon?"

Mama Lil smiled. "Anytime. I'll write down my phone number for you."

Embracing Mama Lil again, Angel thanked her.

Dom expressed his condolences. "Ms. Fox was always nice to me."

I stared at Dom, and wondered why I didn't remember Ms. Fox. The name sounded familiar, but I had no memory of her.

"Thanks," Angel told my brother before she met my eyes again. "Well, I hope to talk to you soon?"

"I can come by tomorrow," I offered. "If you want."

"Sure. I should be there most of the day." She pulled out her business card and slid it over to me. "Call me before you come."

"I will." I looked at Mehki and held up my hand. He gave me a high five. "I'll see you tomorrow, Lil Man."

"Awesome!" He took off toward the booth where their group was seated.

"He has a lot of energy," Angel explained. "I'll let you get back to your meal." She looked at Mama Lil and Dom. "It was nice to meet you both."

"I look forward to talking to you again, sweetie," Mama Lil said. "We're open seven days a week. Stop by for a hot meal when you don't feel like cooking."

"I will. See you soon, Cooper."

Then, she walked away. And I watched her until she slid into the corner booth. When I turned to Mama Lil and Dom, they were both staring at me with knowing glances. "What?"

"Mmmhmm." Mama Lil folded her arms across her chest. "You like her."

"You might be on to something, Mama Lil." Dom

sprinkled salt and pepper over his omelet. “I think I just met the reason your ass didn’t get on that plane.”

“Shut the hell up,” I grumbled, cutting into my pancakes. “I just met her.”

“Whatever you say, CooCoo.” Mama Lil waved her hand at him. “I have to get out of here, boys. Come back and see me before you leave.” She headed over to the corner booth where Angel was seated with her family.

“Say what you will,” Dom said as he chewed a big piece of his omelet, “but if you’re still here next week I’ll know what’s up.”

“Don’t play me, man. I told you… Granddad asked me to restore the house.”

Dom paused, fork in midair. “Ms. Fox’s house?”

“Yes.”

“That’s… weird.”

“I thought the same thing. But that’s not the point. If I’m supposed to restore the Fox house, Angel is the person I need to work with to get that done. That’s all.”

Even as I said that, I knew it wasn’t entirely true. Because Angel Crawford was definitely someone I wanted to get to know.

“WHAT’S UP, MAN?” I switched my phone from one ear to the next, pulled out my keycard, and opened the door to my room.

“Working.” Preston shouted to someone that he was walking away for a minute. Seconds later, he said, “Shit, I should’ve stayed my ass in the office. Working outside in this windchill is a bitch.”

Preston Hayes was my best friend and business partner. He’d left his corporate job as an architect to jump in with me on my mission to become a game changer in the construction business. We'd developed and built several prominent buildings in the Detroit area. Currently, we'd invested a lot of capital to build and rehab homes for low-income residents. Giving back to the Black community was more important to me than being a corporate suit. Not that Prescott Holdings didn't help the community. It was actually quite the opposite. The company had spent millions in its philanthropic endeavors through the years. Granddad had insisted on doing whatever they could to ease the struggle of Rosewood Heights residents and beyond. He felt it was his responsibility to help others rise above the circumstances that were always at play for Black people in America. That was one of the most important lessons he'd taught me.

"How's everything going at the site?" I asked.

"Everything is fine. Why are you still in Rosewood Heights?"

I'd asked myself that same damn question at least a hundred times since I'd arrived two weeks ago. I kicked off my boots and scanned the room. While the suite was comfortable, it wasn't home. Although I'd done it on more than one occasion, my ass was old and cranky, and I hated living out of a suitcase. I needed a kitchen, a firm bed, and space to do shit other than sit on stiff furniture and watch T.V.

"I have some things to take care of here," I explained.

"Everything good?"

"Yeah." I picked up the remote and turned on the television. After I scrolled through a few channels I turned it off. "I'll be back soon." *Or not.* I still couldn't understand why I didn't just hire the contractors for the home restoration and get the hell out town. "I need a favor, though."

"What's up?"

"I have a project that needs to get done as soon as possible." I shared the details about my grandfather's request. "Unfortunately, the woman who owned the house died shortly after Granddad, but her great-niece is in charge of her estate."

"Ah, okay. Is she interested in keeping the house? Or selling?"

"We haven't really talked about it yet, but I plan to meet with her today."

"Alright. Send me the schematics when you can. I'll get started right away."

I thought about the timeline for completion. The house had good bones. I'd peeped a few structural details while I was there, and I'd done some research on the property. "I'll send you pictures, measurements, and the county records I pulled."

"Any thoughts on budget?" Preston asked.

"Not right now. But I'm not going to shortchange this. I want everything to be top quality, including the contractors. I've reached out to several local people already. I also have a plug on a landscaping company that my family has used for years. But I'm not opposed to flying some of our guys down to get the job done."

"I'll put out feelers," Preston told me. "We're pretty slow due to the weather. A lot of our guys are looking for extra work."

"Good. Keep me posted. If all goes according to plan, we should be able to start next week."

"Does this mean you're down there for the foreseeable future?"

I sank into the chair and kicked my feet up. Preston and I had met while we were both Marines stationed in Germany. There wasn't much he didn't know about me, and I knew I could trust him with my life. So, I told him everything.

"Damn, bruh," Preston said. "I'd say you got a dilemma."

"For real."

"I know how much Granddad meant to you, so I can't tell you to ignore his request. I *can* tell you that he's right. You can do both easily."

Rubbing my head, I said, "I'm not so sure about that. Do I really want to uproot my life and move back to Rosewood Heights? Run a company that I'd tried so hard to divest myself from?"

"You're a board member. So you haven't completed divested yourself from Prescott Holdings, man."

"Still… I love what I do."

"Listen, bruh, this isn't something that has to feel like a death sentence. Your father isn't retired yet, and his succession plan can give you as long as you need to handle your shit here. I'm pretty sure no one expects you to take over tomorrow. And I don't think you have to leave Prescott-Hayes Construction completely to be an effective leader at Prescott Holdings."

"I don't know, man. My father…"

"…is going to be your father. He's who he has always been. So are you. Y'all may never get along, but don't let that keep you from honoring the man who supported you through everything you wanted to do. Trust me, it's not easy living with that regret if you don't."

Preston had lost his father at a young age, and he'd struggled with the regret of their last conversation since then. The sudden death had changed his entire life and propelled his path forward in both good and dangerous ways.

"I hear you, bruh," I acknowledged. "It's a lot to think about."

"Not really. You know what to do. And you know I got you. Prescott-Hayes will be ours no matter where *you* live. I actually think an expansion might be good for our bottom line."

Laughing, I said, "Now, you're going too far."

"You know we dream big and in color. Nothing is *too* far."

I glanced at my watch. "Whatever. I got shit to do. I'll send you what you need tonight."

Ending the call, I thought about Pres' words. Nothing he'd said was outrageous. And for the first time, I considered finding a more permanent place in town. I told myself that it made sense to have a house in Rosewood Heights for visits. I knew there was more to it than that, though. But I didn't know if it was Granddad's voice or my own heart at this point.

Chapter 3

ANGEL

"Stop running, Mehki!"

"Angel? Girl, what is all this stuff?" My best friend Tierra pointed to the mounds of boxes near the front door.

I closed a huge, plastic bin full of old hats. "It's everything from Aunt Lou's apartment."

Aunt Lou had resided in an assisted living community for the last few years of her life. With her health challenges, it was easier for her to live in a smaller space where everything was on one floor. The Rosewood Pines staff had been amazing, and so helpful to me, as I'd gathered Auntie's belongings. A few of the nurse assistants had even offered to help me clean out the big house.

I sighed and dropped several purses into an empty bin. "This is a lot of shit," I murmured.

Tierra approached me. "You've been going non-stop, sis. You even worked yesterday after the memorial."

The short, yet emotional ceremony yesterday had drained me. But being in the house, working on finalizing Aunt Lou's affairs, had centered me. I felt at home here. Mehki and I were still staying at the inn, but I'd considered just staying in the house.

"If I don't do it, who will?" I raised a questioning brow. "Mom and Dad couldn't wait to go home. So, I'm it. I already let Aunt Lou down by not actually sitting with her to hear her plans, and I won't walk away from this now."

Shrugging, my friend said, "Okay, then. You got me for the rest of the day. What can I help with?"

"Basement or kitchen?"

She frowned, placing a hand on her hip. "I'm not stepping foot in that dungeon by myself. We can tag team." She peered up at the ceiling, "But this house reminds me of a horror movie. I can imagine all kinds of scary shit happening here. Hauntings, ghosts… demons."

Back in elementary school, Tierra had refused to go trick or treating because she swore Michael Myers lived in the house on the corner of our street. We couldn't go to any bonfires or haunted hay rides with our classmates because my friend was terrified of trees in moonlight. Go figure.

I laughed. "Girl, please!"

A loud thump sounded from the sunroom and Tierra screamed. "See!" She pointed toward the hallway. "You heard that shit. I'm telling you… You saw that movie, *The Conjuring*. That's how it starts. Loud sounds, creaky stairs at night… On second thought, how about we hire people to pack up?"

"Tee!" I shook my head. "That's Mehki. He's in the sunroom working on some experiment with sunlight and plants. And you need to stop watching that shit if you're going to be paranoid about every damn thing."

Tierra grumbled something under her breath and picked up an empty box. "How about I just put this together?" she suggested. "I can be your box and tape girl."

Rolling my eyes, I told her, "Nah, Tee. If you're going to stay, you can be that kitchen girl. Take yo' ass in there and starting packing."

She laughed. "Oh, so it's like that."

"Hell yeah."

"I figured the kitchen would be something we could do together?" She shrugged. "I missed you."

We'd grown up more like sisters, but we were polar opposites on mostly everything. While I loved being outside, Tee enjoyed controlled air and rarely opened her windows. I enjoyed playing *and* watching sports, but she hated to sweat and be around loud noise. I excelled at math, and she flourished in art and design. Sweatpants, protective hairstyles, and comfortable shoes were my preferred look while she wore a full face of makeup, bling, and high heels every day. But I loved her bougie ass. Tierra hated to get dirty, but she'd take off her diamond earrings to cut a bitch—or a nigga—if she had to for me. And I wouldn't hesitate to do the same. We were to each other what I'd always imagined sisters would be, and I wouldn't trade our relationship for anything.

I grabbed the bubble wrap and a box. Then, I walked into the kitchen. "Girl, come on."

She followed me into the room and we started emptying cabinets quietly. After a few minutes, she asked, "Do you think your Aunt Lou wanted you to sell this place?"

That very question had dogged me since I'd arrived in Rosewood Heights. The informal will reading had been enlightening. Aunt Lou had made a small fortune, investing in various businesses over the years, and she'd left almost everything to me. A large sum of money, the house, a smaller beach house in Florida I didn't know about, all of her rental properties, her clothes, her jewelry… The only thing she'd left my mother were a few family heirlooms, a necklace my grandmother had given her, and an apartment in Charleston.

I'd always led a comfortable life. Both of my parents had high-powered careers and they'd given me—their only child—a good life. They'd both instilled in me a desire to work for what I wanted, and I'd held a job from the age of fifteen when I worked as an usher at the local movie theater. After college, I'd been deliberate in my career trajectory, working my way up from an Accounting Assistant to my current position as Director of Budget for a university medical school. At thirty-five, I considered myself a successful Black woman. Suddenly, I was a *rich*, Black woman with enough money to never put on a power suit and go to work again. Every time I thought about it, I became more overwhelmed with all the options I didn't have last month.

"Angel?"

Tierra's voice pulled me from my thoughts and I shrugged. "I actually think she wants me to keep the house."

Her eyes widened. "Seriously? What would you do with it? Just let it sit here and collect dust? The money you'd have to spend on upkeep would be… Shit, that's a lot."

My friend had no idea Aunt Lou had left me everything. "Not really. She left me practically everything."

Her mouth fell open.

"And let me just say it's more than enough to handle the upkeep of this home and more"

"Wow, sis!" Her whole face lit up. "That's pretty awesome. I'm happy for you. Maybe you can stop working so damn hard and live a little?"

"Don't start," I grumbled. These days, every talk with Tee ended with her telling me to let my hair down and experience life.

"Angel." She stepped over to me and grabbed my hands. "I'm so serious. It's time you get some."

My head whipped to the door, hoping Mehki was nowhere near this conversation. "Tee! Mehki?" I added in a whisper.

She shot me an annoyed look. "My godson is in his happy place right now. This is between me and you."

"Still…" My shoulders fell. "I don't want him hearing about his momma 'getting some'. He remembers everything."

"And I'm sure he will also remember his momma never doing anything other than work and taking care of him," she retorted. "Sis, getting some doesn't just mean sex—although you definitely need some dick. You need to have some fun."

"I have fun," I argued. "We go shopping, we go to the movies… That last book club we had was amazing!"

Tee glared at me. "That's old woman fun. And I only do that shit because you love it. I'm talking about traveling, dancing." She bumped my hip. "Double dates and cruises on a yacht."

"You know I have Mehki. I have to be there for him. I'm his only parent."

"You *are* there for him. You've *been* there for him. You'll *continue* to be there for him. But what happens when he's grown and wants to get married?"

The thought of my baby having a baby made my chest hurt. He was so little, so needy. "I guess I'll be there with bells on. As long as he's happy."

"What about *your* happiness?"

"I'll be happy if he's happy," I insisted, pulled my hands from hers. Opening a lower cabinet, I pulled out a cake pan and set it on the counter. "Look, I'm fine."

"You could be better, sis." I felt her approach me. She laid her head on my back and hugged me. "I worry about you."

Turning, I asked, "Why?"

"Because my friend is letting her life pass her by. I know Malachi's death was tough." She wiped a tear from her cheek. "It was devastating."

My heartbeat pounded in my ears as tears welled up in my eyes. Talking about Malachi and the accident and the aftermath was a touchy subject for me, even seven years later. The fact that he never even knew I was pregnant, that I couldn't even tell him the good news after we'd tried for such a long time, felt like a weight in my gut that never let up. What should have been a carefree, happy pregnancy turned into a traumatic, grief-filled time of regret and overwhelming sorrow. It was Mehki that brought back light into my darkness, joy back into my heart. I vowed to be everything he needed from the moment I looked into his big brown eyes.

"You're an awesome mother," Tee said. "Mehki is intelligent, handsome, gifted, funny… He's so many things, and that's because of *you*. And I know Malachi would agree with me."

I shook my head, averting my gaze. "You don't know what Malachi would think."

"I do. We all grew up together. I'm the one who pushed him to ask you to Homecoming. I know that he would want you to be happy. That doesn't mean you forget him, but it does mean you give yourself some grace and let someone in."

I thought about my late husband, my first love every day. Malachi loved me. He *would* want me to be happy. I knew that. I *felt* that in my bones. Still, I could never bring myself to make that move, to accept a date, to even allow myself to be attracted to another man. *Until Cutie Prescott.*

Cooper had stepped into Aunt Lou's house with his dimpled smile and mysterious, dark eyes, and I felt genuine attraction to another man. It had been a long time. Part of me wondered if it was because Mehki seemed to be drawn to him. Part of me knew it was because *I* felt a surprise connection to him. But the thought of opening myself up again scared the shit out of me.

I'm sick of thinking about this. Shaking my mind free of those thoughts, I said, "It's not the right time, Tee. Besides, I'm content."

"I got a job offer," she announced. "Actually, a business opportunity. To partner with Jessica Austin on her new interior design business."

I gasped, smiling. "That's great, Tee! It's your dream. You were holding out on me."

"I'd have to move to California," she confessed.

My heart dropped. Tee was an integral part of my support system. She lived minutes away from us, and she was always there when I needed her. And Cali was far. "That's good." I tried to keep my voice upbeat. "It's what you've always wanted."

"I haven't taken it yet."

Frowning, I said, "What? Why wouldn't you take it? You've worked so hard."

Tee had been a realtor for years, but she'd built a pretty impressive business designing on the side. It was her passion, and I really was elated that she'd been blessed with the opportunity to take her skills to another level.

"Because." She shrugged. "What will you do if I'm not here?"

I fought back tears, but they fell anyway. The fact that my friend was holding back on her dream for me was too much to bear. I walked away and hurried to the half bathroom near the front door. Staring at myself in the mirror, I noted the raccoon look that I wasn't going for when I'd put on mascara and eye liner that morning. *Is this really what my life has become?*

"Angel?"

I glanced at Tee through the mirror. She stood, arms folded across her chest, tears in her eyes. "I'm okay," I assured her. "Just been an emotional week. Or two."

"Or five?"

I giggled. "Right. Seriously? Take the offer. Don't worry about me. Me and Mehki will be just fine. That's why we have planes." I raised my brows. "We could come visit; help you find a place… It'll be good for you."

She sniffled. "I'm going to take it. *If* you promise to do better, sis. I need you to be okay."

Turning to face her, I smiled. "We'll be okay." I hugged her. "We all will."

After a moment, I pulled away and checked out my reflection again. "What time is it?"

"Almost noon. Why?"

I gasped. "Shit!" I rushed into the living room and grabbed my purse. Then, hurried back to the bathroom.

Tee stared at me, a slack expression on her face. "What the hell is wrong with you?"

"Cutie Prescott will be here soon, and I look like this." I gestured to my face.

Grinning, she tilted her head. "And?"

I fumbled in my makeup bag for my mascara. "I don't want to look crazy when he gets here. We have business to talk about."

"Mmmhmm."

I raised my hands at my sides. "What?"

"I noticed the way you looked at him at that restaurant yesterday." She raised a challenging brow. "He *is* fine."

"I told you he was fine." After I met Cooper, I'd told Tierra about the visit. "I do call him Cutie Prescott."

"Yeah, but I don't even remember you ever caring about your makeup like this."

"Of course I care." I let out a strained giggle, as heat crept up my neck to my cheeks. "I always want to look presentable."

"Mmmhmm," she repeated.

"Mommie!" Mehki yelled. "Mr. Cooper's here."

"Okay!" I shouted. "I'll be right there."

I dug into my bag, cursing when I didn't find my eyeliner. Peering into the bag, I finally located it and pulled it out. When I glanced in the mirror, Tee was still watching me with an amused smile on her face. "Stop staring and help me," I begged.

She jumped into action, swatting my hands away and taking over the makeup duties. "Just so you know," she said, "we're not done talking about this. But I'm not going to let you go out like a punk."

"Thank you!"

Several minutes later, I emerged from the bathroom, face fixed. The door was open, but there was no sign of Mehki or Cooper. Panic rose in me as I raced to the front door, calling my son's name.

"Meh—!" I froze when I spotted my son outside, his head down, staring at the ground. Next to him, Cooper was on his knees, pointing to the grass.

"Angel, what…?" Tee stopped next to me. "What the hell are they doing?"

At first I wasn't sure, but it was clear the two of them were looking at some sort of insect. I studied them, noting the way Mehki's face brightened when Cooper told him something. My son clapped with glee, jumped up and down, then held out his hand just in time to let Cooper drop what was most likely a spider into it.

"I don't know," I murmured, watching them approach the door. The unmistakable delight on Mehki's face hadn't faded the entire way up the sidewalk. Cooper seemed to have a way with him, and it warmed my heart. *I might be in trouble.*

Cooper held back and allowed Mehki to step on the porch first. "Hi," he said, his voice smooth, deep.

The sound bypassed my fluttering stomach and went straight to my pussy. "Hi," I croaked.

Mehki tugged at my shirt, effectively pulling me out of my Cooper haze. "Mommie!"

I met my baby's dancing eyes. "Yes, babe?"

"Mr. Cooper helped me catch a spider," he exclaimed, his wide grin still on display. "I thought it was a Harvest-men, but Mr. Cooper told me it was a Cellar Spider."

I frowned. "A… Cellar Spider?"

"A Daddy Long Legs," Cooper offered.

"Oh," I muttered.

"Harmless," he added.

Clutching the charm on my necklace, I nodded. "Babe, let's leave the spider outside, okay?"

Mehki's smile fell. "Aw, but I wanted to keep it."

"You can keep it, but it has to stay outside," I told him.

"Um," Tee chimed in. "I think I saw an empty aquarium inside. Maybe he can put it in there?"

I gave my friend a skeptical look, because one thing we

could agree on was that bugs and spiders deserved to be killed as soon as possible. "Really?" I lifted an eyebrow. "Are you going to help him put it in there?"

Tee let out a strained giggle, glanced at Cooper and said, "No. But I'm sure *he* will. I'm Tierra Willis, by the way."

Cooper shook Tee's outstretched hand. "Cooper Prescott." He looked at me. "I'll get the spider settled for you. No worries."

"Be my guest." I waved a hand, gesturing for him to take over the spider duties.

"DO YOU HAVE EVERYTHING YOU NEED?" I slid a bottle of water over to Cooper, who was typing furiously on his phone. It had been a few hours since he'd arrived. After he'd safely secured Mehki's spider, he walked me through his process, giving me a verbal outline of what I could expect during construction—*if* I chose to let him to do the job.

We spent much of the time touring the house. He'd taken measurements, snapped pictures, and talked about construction-related things. None of it was foreign to me because Malachi had owned a construction company. I knew all about zoning, box cribs, drywall, and weight-bearing columns among other things.

Cooper thanked me for the water. "I think so. Once my architect reviews everything, we can get started on the design elements if you choose to let me do the job."

He keeps saying that. Through everything, he'd made sure he reiterated that none of this would happen without my approval. I liked that about him. He wasn't a typical man, trying to overtalk me and patronize me. He seemed to pick up on the fact that I knew a little something, so he shot straight, spouting off costs and giving loose estimates for certain materials.

"I'm thinking we can get to work next week if you're in agreement," he added. "Barring any delays with the work permits."

Again, he'd made sure I knew it was my decision. Although his grandfather had asked him to do the job, I loved that Cooper wasn't pushing the issue.

Unable to help myself, I smiled. It wasn't the first time either. And it wasn't just simple smiles here or there. Apparently, I liked to giggle in Cooper's presence, too. *He's so funny!* His sense of humor put me at ease quickly.

I glanced over at Tee, who'd been watching me intently, a sneaky smile on her lips. Straightening my face, I shot her a death glare and a soundless command to "get out." Because I knew what my friend was thinking, and I refused to go there.

She stood up quickly. "I'm going to check on Mehki." She waved. "Be right back."

Once she'd left the room, I slid into the chair next to Cooper. His cologne was working its magic on me again. Today, he smelled like lemons and mint. I tried to ignore the compulsion to sit closer. "So listen…" I cleared my throat. "I must admit I'm a little intrigued." *Damnit.* If I could go back and reword that sentence I would. It felt like I'd stepped onto a mine field, because I couldn't decide if I was intrigued by the project itself or him.

He tossed me a little half-smirk. "Care to elaborate?"

I blinked, snapping my attention away from his lips. "Oh." I released a shaky breath. "Um… About this business between my Aunt Lou and your grandfather."

His tongue darted out to lick his lips and he leaned in. "Honestly?" he murmured.

Like a moth to a flame, I moved closer, too. "Yes."

"I think they had something going on."

My mouth fell open. "No." I pulled back. "No way."

Nodding, he said, "Oh yeah. Speaking as a man, I'm not going to restore someone's house if I didn't have a past—or a future—with them. One that includes sex."

A nervous laugh burst free. "Really?" The question came out more sultry than curious.

"Damn straight."

I stared at Aunt Lou's portrait again, and wondered if Cooper's grandfather was the man that had made her so happy in it. "You might have point," I mused, giving him a sidelong glance. "I say we do some digging."

"Sounds like a plan."

Our gazes locked. The intensity in his dark eyes was turning me inside out. Forcing myself to look away, I stood and ventured over to the picture window in the front of the house. "There are some personal things I still have to go through. I think I'll do that tonight."

"Good." He joined me at the window. "*If* you decide to move forward, you'll need to move to another location, maybe a short-term rental. We'll need to clear everything out."

"I'm not staying here now," I admitted.

"Mind if I ask why?"

With a shrug, I explained, "I'm not sure, actually. If you really want the truth, I figured I'd be back home by now."

"Charleston, right?"

"Yeah. This trip to Rosewood Heights has been more than I ever expected."

He arched a brow. "Let me ask you… are you okay with the renovation?"

"Definitely. Your grandfather promised to do this for

my aunt. It was obviously something *she* wanted, so I want it, too."

"Good to know. I do want some of my contractors to come in and do an extensive inspection. I need to know what I'm looking at, if there are any structural repairs that need to be done."

We hadn't talked the budget yet, so I asked, "When can you send me a quote? I want to prepare for the expense."

"Don't worry about it."

"I have to," I argued. "This is what I do. I'm all about the money."

"What *do* you do?" he asked, ignoring my question again.

The business card I'd given him at the restaurant had little about me other than my name and phone number. I'd made them once I realized I'd have to handle Aunt Lou's affairs. I shared my title with him, and then went on to offer more details than he'd asked. Absently, I wondered why I felt comfortable telling him so much about my life. But this man seemed to bring out things in me that I thought I'd tamped down years ago. For the longest time, I identified solely as Mehki's mother, Director of Budget, Friend of Tierra, and Daughter of Benjamin and Theresa Holloway. Yet, with Cooper, I felt like a woman. And the way he looked at me made me feel like an *attractive* woman, a *desirable* woman. Surprisingly, that was a welcome feeling, one I couldn't say I didn't want to experience more of.

"I'm thinking of taking a leave of absence," I babbled on, "to take care of everything here, and spend some time with Mehki." *Shit, Angel, you didn't even say that to Tee.* I tugged on my shirt. "And you can feel free to tell me to be quiet if I'm talking too much." I wanted to tell myself to shut the hell up.

His gaze dropped to my mouth. "Why would I do that?"

Instinctively, I rubbed my bottom lip with my thumb. *Damn, I forgot my lip gloss.* I licked my lips and prayed they didn't look ashy. "Because… we just met. It's weird for me to talk to this much."

He laughed. "You're not. If you were, it wouldn't bother me. I like your voice."

Releasing my bottom lip, I stepped away from him. Distance was necessary.

"Okay." I didn't know what to say to that shit. No one had ever told me they liked my voice, not even Malachi.

"Do you sing?" he asked.

"Sometimes. But not very well." It was a lie. I'd been singing my entire life. Not just in the shower either. I'd traveled with choirs, recorded with producers, and had even written a few songs. I still sang to Mehki, but anything other than Dream a Little Dream and other lullabies had stopped when Malachi died.

"Why don't I believe you?"

"I have no idea." I shrugged. "Maybe you're just a naturally suspicious person."

Chuckling, he admitted, "That's kind of true."

"See!"

"But you sound like you can sing. The inflections in your voice, the tone… almost melodic. Soft."

Shit. He's good. "Well, congratulations. You've officially rendered me speechless."

He smiled. "You crack me up."

If only it was that simple for me. Yes, he made me laugh, but he also made me… hot. And very bothered. "Thanks."

Struggling with my conflicting emotions and tempted

to say something that might get me in trouble, I breathed a sigh of relief when Mehki barreled into the room.

An out of breath Tee entered the room seconds later. Leaning against the table, she mouthed a quick apology and muttered, “He’s so damn fast.”

“Mommie, I’m hungry,” Mehki said. “Can I have a grilled cheese and soup?”

I eyed Cooper out of the corner of my eye. *Yep, he’s still watching me.* “Sure, honey.” I grabbed Mehki’s hand. I’d picked up a few groceries from the store because I knew we’d be spending a lot of time at the house. “I can make that for you right now.” Turning to Cooper, I asked, “Do you mind?”

“Only if you make me some, too.”

With narrowed eyes, I asked, “Why do I think you’re going to be a handful?”

He grinned. “I don’t know. Maybe it’s because you’re a naturally suspicious person.”

I laughed. Loud. Then, I realized that Tee and Mehki were watching me with interest. Drawing in a deep breath, I told Cooper, “That’s actually very true.”

“Then, I guess we have something in common.”

It had become very clear that we had more than a few things in common. In that moment, I realized that I wanted to find out more about Cooper Prescott.

Chapter 4

COOPER

Maverick gave me a dap. "What? You still here?"

"You still a dumb ass?" I tossed back, annoyed at the constant jokes from my family about my extended time in Rosewood Heights. It had been nearly a month since the funeral, and I was still here. I'd only ventured back to Detroit to get more clothes and my truck, before high-tailing it back down to South Carolina.

"Man, shut yo' ass up."

I shrugged. "Just sayin'."

He waved me off. "Get the hell out of here."

Laughing, I squeezed his shoulder. "I live to piss you off."

Back in the day, Maverick was an easy target. He'd played his role as the skinny, nerdy little brother to a tee. Making fun of him seemed like a requirement. Being the second oldest—Hunter was four minutes younger—had its perks. Although I would beat a nigga down for my brothers, I didn't have to protect them from each other like Dom did. Poor Mav didn't stand a chance.

"Whatever, asshole." Mav poured a glass of lemonade. "Mom told me you decided to buy a condo."

Shaking my head, I pulled out a glass. "Rented," I corrected. "I *rented* a condo."

Instead of lemonade, I went with the cognac. Especially since I'd come to the house specifically to talk to my father. For the first time since the funeral, Dad had actually texted me and asked for a meeting. My response had morphed from "hell no" to "maybe next week" to "what time". I just added my change of heart about having a conversation with my father to the list of things I'd said I wouldn't do since Granddad died.

"Either way, it's surprising," Mav said. "What's the end game? Are you actually considering taking your place beside us at the company?"

Weeks ago, the answer to that question would have been a no, unequivocally. But now? *I'm a fuckin' punk.* I gulped the alcohol down. "Don't read too much into this." I set the glass on the counter and poured another healthy serving. "I'm working on a special project for Granddad."

"Oh yeah… I heard you were remodeling the Fox house."

I stared at him. "Who told you?"

"It's Rosewood Heights. Everybody pretty much knows what everybody else is doing."

I leaned against the counter. "Did you know Ms. Fox?"

Mav frowned. "Not really. I've seen her around."

"I don't remember her," I mused. I'd studied the portrait of her at the house, but I didn't recall ever running into her. Which was weird, since I'd lived in this damn town until I was eighteen.

"That's not surprising. You've been gone for a long time."

"But I remember a lot of things about this place. Just not her."

"I don't know, bruh." Maverick finished his lemonade. "When do you start on the project?"

Between the inspections, the design, and the permit process, I had to push the start date back. "Hopefully, tomorrow."

"How long do you think it will take?"

I hunched a shoulder. The 5,500-square-foot house was built in 1925, so I'd anticipated unexpected delays. "My goal is to be finished by Memorial Day."

"What happens when you're done?" Hunter walked into the kitchen and greeted me and Mav with a bro hug. "I can't believe you're still here."

"I can't believe no one in this family knows how to mind their own damn business," I snapped. "Stop worrying about why I'm here and concentrate on your own shit. Damn."

Hunter grinned. "Whoa, can't a brotha ask a question?"

"Apparently not," Mav muttered.

I could have clapped back, but I chose a different tactic. "How you feeling today, bruh?" I asked my twin.

"Ready to be back to where I was."

"Maybe then you can buy some food for your place," I told him.

Dom had us visiting Hunter five minutes after his plane landed the other day, during dinner hours, with nothing good to eat.

"I have food," Hunter argued. "*My* food. You can buy *your* food for *your* place, since I heard you bought a condo."

I groaned. "Mom needs to get her damn story straight."

Mav opened the refrigerator. "Y'all want to grab something to eat?"

"That'll work," Hunter said. "Coop?"

My agenda consisted of stopping by the Fox house to drop some of my tools off and trying to finagle a dinner invitation from Angel. Mehki had been right. The woman could cook. She'd made the hell out of those grilled cheese sandwiches. And since then, she'd had something delicious for me—*I mean, Mehki*—every time I'd seen her. It had been a long time since I'd spent so much time with an attractive woman—other than Dallas—where sex wasn't involved. I almost didn't know what to do with myself, because—unlike with Dallas—I *wanted* there to be sex involved.

Angel was a beautiful woman. Sexy, intelligent, interesting… She definitely left me wanting more. The idea of getting close to her didn't even scare me as much as it should have. She *was* someone's mother. I'd been careful not to hook up with women who had young children. Not because I didn't like kids. I loved them, but I didn't relish breaking their hearts when I left their moms.

"I think I have plans," I answered, glancing at my watch.

Hunter raised a questioning brow. "You think?"

"What's with all the questions?" I held out my arms. "Mav wants to know my construction schedule; you want to know my thoughts… Maybe I *should* take my ass back to Detroit as soon as possible." I wasn't serious, but I also wasn't ready to talk about anything Angel-related with my brothers. That included the Fox house.

"Shit, man…" Mav shook his head. "I'll keep my questions to myself."

I glanced at Mav, then at Hunter. And now I felt bad. Rosewood Heights had not only brought out my punk tendencies, but it also made me soft. I didn't like it. At all. "I have a lot of shit to do, that's all," I explained lamely. "I'm frustrated."

Hunter slid onto a stool. "Need help with anything?"

"Nah. I'll handle it, bruh."

"Since I didn't agree to keep my questions to myself," Hunter said, "I have to ask… Are you frustrated because of the work or because you don't want to be here?"

"Both," I blurted out. "Neither."

"Which one is it?"

Sighing, I took a sip from my glass. "I love what I do. I'm all in on this project. I'm also not upset that I'm here. Which is frustrating as fuck because I haven't wanted to be in Rosewood Heights in a lot of years, and I'm trying to figure out why the hell I'm in no hurry to leave." I hadn't expected to lay it all out on the table like that, but I needed to get it out.

"Time is a hell of a drug," Mav offered. "One minute, we're living our lives without reservations or regrets. The next, we're moving heaven and earth to do everything we said we wouldn't. I feel like it's just the way it goes."

Hunter pointed at our little brother. "You said a mouthful, bruh."

"That *was* deep," I admitted.

Mav grinned. "I'm good like that."

"Don't get carried away. You're still a dumb ass." I cracked up when Mav gave me the middle finger. Glancing at my watch, I said, "I better get out of here. I need to go talk to Dad."

"What?" they both said at the same time, each of them with a look of surprise on their faces.

Ignoring them, I walked out of the room and shouted, "Mind your business."

Minutes later, I was seated in front of my father. The office looked like I'd remembered—large furniture, white walls, pictures of the family on the shelves of the bookcase. And just like the last time I was there, the tension was palpable.

"You wanted to see me?" I asked.

Dad stared at me for a moment, before he answered. "Yes, I wanted to talk to you about a few things."

I waited for him to continue. When he didn't, I said, "Okay?"

Leaning forward, he slid a large manilla envelope toward me. "I found this in your grandfather's things. It's addressed to you."

I made no move to open the envelope. "You called me here for this?"

"I know you're restoring Louise Fox's home."

"I was under the impression Granddad didn't share his requests with anyone."

Shrugging, my father said, "He told me about *this* project. He knew that the cost of the renovations might be more than he'd given you to complete it. So I've been instructed to see to it that you have everything you need."

Another piece to the puzzle. "What is it about Louise Fox? Was she involved with Granddad? Did he have an affair with her?"

Dad dropped his gaze. "I don't know. He never talked to me about her."

The thought that Granddad had cheated on Granny with Louise didn't feel right to me. But nothing about this made any sense. Angel hadn't discovered anything either. "I'm a little confused as to why he wanted me to do this."

"You're not the only one," he mumbled.

I took a moment to study my father. He looked… tired. Sad. "Are you okay?"

The question must have caught him off guard because he slumped back in his seat and let out a heavy sigh. "He was my father. I loved him. I worked hard for him my entire life. Now, he's gone."

The admission filled the space of the room, his sorrow potent, raw. I knew Granddad had a special relationship with all of his grandchildren, but I'd never stopped to think about the relationship he had with my father.

Swallowing, I said, "It can't be easy for you."

His eyes flashed to mine. "It's not."

The statement hung in the air. I didn't know how to respond to that. I'd seen my father angry and disappointed, sometimes even happy. He displayed confidence at all times and never showed weakness. He was a pillar of strength, unbreakable and unwavering in his convictions. But this… I'd never seen my dad look so lost. Not even when Granny died.

"Your grandfather was right," he admitted softly.

I didn't want to assume I'd heard him right, so I asked, "What did you say?"

"He was right about you. Your accomplishments? None of them were unexpected. From the very beginning, I knew you would surpass my expectations."

Unbelievable.

"I'm not going to force you," Dad continued. "But I do agree that it's time for you to come home and work with us at Prescott Holdings."

The compulsion to argue or make up an excuse to leave was strong in that moment. But I couldn't move.

Dad opened a drawer and pulled out leather-bound folder. "This is the company portfolio. As a board member, you already received one. I don't know if you've read it, but I'd like you take a look." He held it out for me. "Maybe we can meet for lunch next week to discuss your plans?"

Maverick's words filtered through my mind. *One minute, we're living our lives without reservations or regrets. The next, we're moving heaven and earth to do everything we said we wouldn't.* I knew I was at a crossroads, stuck between doing what I loved and stepping into a role I'd never wanted.

I took the folder. And instead of telling my father no, I said, "Just tell me when."

Chapter 5

ANGEL

"Mr. Cooper!" Mehki took off running.

"Mom, I have to go. I'll keep you updated." I ended the call with my mother, which had lasted from breakfast through the drive over to the house.

Construction on the house had started several weeks ago. Cooper and his crew were quickly transforming it into a place I couldn't imagine walking away from. Cutie Prescott had been straightforward through the entire process, guiding me through each step and handling any problems that cropped up with ease. They worked swiftly, yet efficiently, which I appreciated tenfold. And I really didn't have to do anything. His team cleared out the house *and* rented a storage unit for everything. He sent daily progress reports that outlined materials installed, explained any safety incidents that slowed down the work, and summarized work completed.

As I neared him standing outside of the house talking to Mehki, my attention was transfixed to his right arm. The sleeve tattoo stretched from his shoulder to his wrist, and had been a source of my admiration since the first time I'd seen it. I wanted to ask questions, but it seemed very inappropriate.

Over the past two months, we'd gotten to know each other a little better. My attraction to him, while still simmering, wasn't as overwhelming as it was initially. I'd grown used to his charming muthafucka ways, and looked forward to the time we would spend together going over plans or eating lunch or even playing with Mehki. Cooper had a way of looking at me that made my toes curl, almost like he was trying to systematically take me apart and examine every piece before he put me back together. The craziest part was that it didn't make me nervous or uncomfortable. I loved it.

"Hey," I said once I'd reached them.

He smiled. "Welcome back, Ms. Crawford. How was Charleston?"

I'd spent much of the last month back home, only returning to Rosewood Heights on the weekends. Mehki missed my parents and Tee. He'd also missed school. Although Mehki's teachers had graciously allowed him to continue his studies remotely while we here for that extended time after Aunt Lou died, he loved being in the classroom. It made sense to stay in Charleston through the school week. Every Friday, we made the trip back to see Coop—Um…the house.

"Great," I said. "I was able to get a lot done, and Mehki took first place at the science fair."

Mehki held up his trophy. "See!"

Cooper held up his hand and Mehki jumped up to give him a high five. "I told you I wouldn't steer you wrong."

"I told my teacher that my project would blow everyone out of the water!"

I laughed. Cooper had used those same words when he'd volunteered to help Mehki with his project. "Some things you shouldn't repeat, babe."

"And some things you should," Cooper said. "Give me another one."

Mehki gave him another high five. "Are you going to show me how to paint now?"

The last time we were at the house, Mehki had been so engrossed with the work being done that he could barely concentrate on his project. So, Cooper promised him he would show him how to paint if he finished his homework.

"You know I will, Lil Man." Cooper eyed me. "When it's time. Does Momma want me to show her how to paint, too?"

A smile tugged at my lips. "No, I think I'm good."

Cooper gave me a rundown of a few last minute changes they'd had to make to the design. "We're making good time. My goal is to start dropping the drywall next week."

"Cool." I stuffed my phone in my purse. "I can't wait until it's done. Did I tell you I decided to relocate?"

His right eyebrow shot up. "No, but I'm not surprised. You act like you love it here."

"I do," I admitted.

It was amazing how this town had endeared itself to me in such a short while. Mehki and I had found an Airbnb that allowed us to rent on the weekends, which enabled us to stretch out a bit on our visits. It wasn't too far from Aunt Lou's house, and Mehki had even met a few neighborhood kids that he enjoyed playing with when we were here. The contrast between city life and small town living, and the peaceful effect this little haven had on our family life, made the decision to relocate easy. I loved the slow pace and the tightknit community, the sweet tea and Mama Lil's pot roast, the sea air and the friendly smiles. The best part was Mehki seemed to love Rosewood Heights as much as I'd grown to love it and couldn't contain his excitement about moving.

"While I was home, I talked to Mehki and my family about it. Everything kind of clicked the last time I was here," I explained. "The intricate details of the design, the additions we talked about … It felt like it was for me, not just a random homebuyer. I can't see myself letting this place go."

The scheduled date of completion coincided with the end of the semester for Mehki, which was ideal. He would be able to finish out the school year in Charleston. My family was on board with my decision, too. Tee had already started the process of putting my house on the market, and we hoped it would sell before my friend made her own move to Los Angeles in June.

Cooper's mouth curved into a smile. "Again, I'm not surprised."

I feigned offense. "Now, you think you know me?"

Laughing, he said, "I think I'm beginning to peep your game."

"Really?" I narrowed my eyes. "Since you think you have me all figured out. What am I thinking now?"

He leaned in. Up close, he was so large and firm and male. I'd yet to touch him in any meaningful way, oven even hug him, but my fingers ached to trace his tattoo, to squeeze the muscles of his biceps, to run my fingers over his smooth brown skin. I wanted to feel his arms around me, then bury my face in his chest. He always smelled so clean, so sexy.

"You're thinking about windows," he whispered.

I barely registered his words because I was so consumed by the feel of his breath against my lips. But when the haze of desire cleared, I blinked, jerking back. "Windows?" Did he mean windows literally or figurately? Charleston Glass Company Windows or windows to my soul?

Chuckling, he said, "New windows. In the house."

I frowned. "Oh. Okay." Confused, and maybe a little annoyed, I followed him into the house. "Be careful, Mehki," I warned.

"Let's start upstairs," Cooper said.

Twenty minutes later, we were back on the porch. "I love that you added the balcony off of the master bedroom. I can already see myself reading or drinking a glass of wine out there."

"I knew you would." Cooper winked. "Told you I peeped your game."

I couldn't stop myself from smiling, but I did cover it up with my hand. "I'm still not convinced."

"I have a few more surprises up my sleeve."

"Now, I'm intrigued."

"Too bad you have to wait until the house is done."

Mehki tapped Cooper. "Do you have any surprises for me?"

Bending down so he was at eye-level with my son, Cooper said, "A lot of surprises."

"Thank you!" Mehki wrapped his arms around Cooper's neck. For his part, Cutie Prescott handled the impromptu hug well, even though he looked slightly uncomfortable. "I'm so happy!"

Tears sprang to my eyes. Aside from my father, Mehki didn't really have any adult men in his life. Seeing him grow so close to Cooper in such a short time warmed my heart. But… *What happens when Cooper goes back home to Detroit?*

Wiping my cheeks, I prayed neither of them saw the tears fall. "Mehki? Are you hungry?"

"Yes!" he cheered.

"What do you want me to cook?" I asked, brushing my hand down his cheek.

"How about we get pizza?" Cooper suggested.

"Mehki doesn't—"

"Pizza!" My son shouted. "I want pizza, Mommie."

Frowning, I said, "You told me you hated pizza, babe."

"I changed my mind," Mehki said with a nod. "Can we go, please?"

I glanced at Cooper, then back at my son. "Okay." Mehki sprinted toward my car. "Be careful, baby." Sighing, I turned to the man who had turned my world upside down in a matter of months. "You started this."

He stepped closer to me. "I'll finish it, too."

Well, damn. My gaze dropped to his mouth. "How?"

A half-smirk, half-smile formed on his lips. "My treat."

I released a slow breath; one I hadn't realized I was holding. "You sure? We eat a lot."

Cooper barked out a laugh. "Not more than me."

An hour later, we were seated at a booth in the local pizzeria. Mehki was happily munching on a huge piece of pizza with three different types of meat.

Leaning forward, I murmured, "How did you get him to eat that?"

"It's man food. He's a lil man." Cooper took a big bite of his slice.

After a few minutes, Mehki asked if he could play the arcade game in the corner. Cooper dug into his jeans and pulled out several quarters before I could say anything. Excited, Mehki raced to the game. One of the waitresses saw him, and set a stool in front of it so he could reach the controls.

I smiled at the glee in his eyes as he glanced back at me before he pushed a coin into the slot and started playing.

"He's a remarkable kid."

Turning my attention to Coop, I said, "He is. I'm so proud of him." I dipped my breadstick into the marinara sauce. "You have a way with kids. Do you spend a lot of time with your niece or nephew?"

"Not as much as my sister wants," he replied. "Before my grandfather died, I didn't make it back to Rosewood Heights often."

"Why?"

He hunched his shoulder. "I didn't want to be here."

"Is that because of your mother and father?" He'd shared a few things about his brothers and his sister, Ava, but very little about his parents.

He leaned back in his seat, assessing me quietly for a moment before he said, "You don't miss much, do you?"

"You don't either."

Cooper stared at me. "For the longest time, I couldn't stand to be in the same room with my father—which often affected my relationship with my mother."

"I'm sorry," I whispered, feeling bad that I'd brought it up. "We don't have to talk about this."

"No, it's fine. Since I've been here, me and my father have had several conversations that didn't involve arguments and accusations. We even had lunch."

"What changed?"

He shifted in his seat. "I guess I have my grandfather to thank for that. His will… The requests he made, flipped everything on its head." He took a sip of his beer. "I think we've come to an understanding of sorts."

"Isn't that a good thing?"

"Maybe. Yes. I don't know."

I giggled. "Well, time is a bipolar bitch. Sometimes it helps, other times it hurts."

Cooper paused. "You sound like you're speaking from experience."

"You don't know the half of it," I murmured.

Mehki ran back to the table. "Mommie, I won! I got a high score." He gave Cooper a fist bump. "I saw your name on the scoreboard. You were number one."

"That's because I'm undefeated." Cooper grabbed another slice of pizza. "I defend my title every time I come to town."

"I'm going to beat you, Mr. Cooper." Mehki slid next to me. "It's my personal mission now."

"You're smart, Lil Man. But I've been kicking butt on that game since I was a kid. I'm not sure you have what it takes to beat me," Cooper teased.

Mehki narrowed his eyes. "I smell a challenge."

I giggled. "Uh oh. You're in trouble, Cooper."

Standing, Cooper pulled a few bucks out of his wallet. "I'm not scared."

They took off toward the game. I watched them play several rounds. I couldn't take my eyes off of the sight in front of me. My son healthy, happy. And Cooper… gentle, fun, and fine.

Later that night, Cooper carried an extremely exhausted Mehki into my house. My son had fallen asleep fast, after ice cream and a trip to the arcade in town.

"Thanks for bringing him in." I dropped my purse on the table. "He gets bigger every day."

"It's probably all that home cooking."

Cooper followed me into the second bedroom of the rental. He gently set Mehki on the bed and pulled off his shoes and baseball cap. I grabbed a pair of pajamas out of the suitcase.

Stretching, Cooper said. "I'll let you handle that."

I smiled. "Give me a few minutes, okay?"

Once Cooper left the room, I removed Mehki's clothes and dressed him in his pajamas. Placing a soft kiss to his forehead, I whispered, "Love you, my sweet boy."

His eyes popped open. "Mommie?" His sleepy voice made my heart melt.

"Yes, babe."

"I'm going to beat Mr. Cooper one day."

Chuckling softly, I said, "I believe you."

"I love you, Mommie."

"Love you, too. Good night."

I flipped the light switch and closed the bedroom door. On my way to the living room, I stopped at the bathroom to check my face. Hair still good, makeup still… *Well, I can't win every battle.* I put a fresh coat of gloss on my lips and went to meet Cooper.

"I think you created a monster." I hung my jacket up. "Mehki is intent on unseating you on that game."

Cooper shrugged. "I have no doubt he'll succeed—one day."

"He's very persistent." I walked over to him. "That day may come sooner than you think."

He smirked. "Like I told you earlier, I'm not scared."

Stopping in front of him, I peered into his dark eyes. "I think I'm looking forward to the day my son wipes that cocky smirk off of your face."

Flashing a sly grin, he whispered, "You might be waiting a long time."

We stood there, nearly touching, eyes locked on one another. The air changed around us and everything seemed to fade away. There was nothing, no sound, no light, just us and this moment. I couldn't control the conflicting emotions swarming through my head. I had to do something, I had to…

Stepping up on the tips of my toes, I kissed him. It wasn't a passionate kiss, but the feel of his mouth against my mouth, his breath mingling with mine calmed the part of me that felt out of control.

But then reality crept in, and the gravity of what I'd just done with my son in the other room, cloaked everything in the shadow of doubt. I'd kissed him. He didn't kiss me. *Did he even want to*?

Jerking away, I took a huge step back. "Um… I… didn't mean… Maybe we should just forget I did that." I swallowed hard and prayed that he would just leave before I embarrassed myself even more.

Cooper inched closer to me. He ran a finger down my cheek, and wrapped his hand around my neck. "I would rather not forget."

Then, *he* kissed me. It was… hot and loaded. His talented mouth devoured mine, tongue and teeth, low groans and bumping chins. Cooper's hands—on my back, on my ass, on my sides, on my face… *Oh Damn.* I didn't want to stop. He could kiss me forever if that meant it would always be like this, if I could always feel so free.

He turned me around so that my back was against the wall. Pressing his hard body into mine, he finally broke the kiss. "I think *you* started something," he murmured, throwing my earlier words back at me. "I'm so tempted." He nipped my ear before sucking the lobe into his mouth.

My breath hitched in my chest when he ran his nose down my neck and bit the base gently. "To do what?" I breathed, gripping his shoulders, holding on for dear life. Because sliding to the ground would not be a good look. Not sexy at all.

"Do more."

"What …?" I blew out a shaky breath. "How much more?"

He met my gaze. His eyes looked like coal, they were so dark. "Too much."

Cooper stepped away from me, leaving me wanting whatever he wanted to give me. I sagged against the wall and tried steadying my breathing. With a hand against my chest, I whispered, "You're probably right. We definitely shouldn't do too much."

"Angel," he said.

I got my shit together and stood up straight. "Yes?"

"I respect you."

Uh oh, this sounds like a letdown.

He drew close to me again. "You're a beautiful woman. Sexy."

Is this the part when he tells me it's not me, it's him?

"I enjoy spending time with you. And Mehki."

The mention of my son's name cleared the fog in my brain. "I feel the same."

"I think…" He tilted his head. "If we want to do *more*, we should take our time."

A wave of relief washed over me. I didn't know what I expected, but I definitely didn't think he would approach this turn of events like this. Nodding, I said, "I agree."

"But I'm so tempted." He brushed his lips over mine. "I better go."

"I think you probably should." I tugged my shirt down and opened the front door. "I'll talk to you soon?"

He walked into the hallway and turned around. "Bye, Angel Crawford."

Leaning against the door, I smiled. "Bye, Cutie Prescott." I slapped my hand over my mouth.

Cooper laughed. Arching a brow, he asked, "Cutie Prescott?"

"Bye, Cooper."

"No, I want to hear more about this."

I pushed him back when he tried to step back into the house. "Bye. Talk to you tomorrow." I closed the door. *Lord, I'm in trouble.*

Chapter 6

COOPER

"Stop asking so many damn questions, Dallas." I entered The Little Rose and nearly ran into Ryleigh.

"Coop?"

I looked down at her baby boy in the stroller. Then, back at her. "What's up, Ryleigh?" I ended the call with Dallas just as she fired off three more questions that I had no intention of answering. I kneeled and spoke to the baby before I stood to my full height. "He's cute. He looks like you."

"Thanks."

"I didn't know you were in town."

"I came to check Mama Lil out," she said, "and go to church with her on Easter Sunday."

"Good. Where is she?"

Ryleigh pointed to the back of the restaurant. "Giving

orders, cooking shit she shouldn't be cooking, and generally being herself." She shrugged. "Some things never change."

"Right." Since I'd been back, I'd spent a lot of time with Mama Lil. "I keep telling her to sit her ass down somewhere."

"I hope you said it just like that."

"I did."

She laughed. "You're probably the only one who could."

"She told me as much, right before she smacked the hell out of me."

Ryleigh cracked up, and I joined her. It felt good to laugh with her again. It had been a long time. "How are you?" she asked.

"Alright."

"Sure?"

The months that I'd been in Rosewood Heights had flown by. The longer I stayed here, the longer I *wanted* to stay. I couldn't deny that had a lot to do with Angel and Mehki. Against my better judgment, I'd become accustomed to seeing them every weekend. In fact, I looked forward to Fridays because I knew they'd be here. Last week, I'd given in to the temptation to taste her, to touch her. And like a fiend, I couldn't wait for my next hit.

"I'm sure," I replied.

"Want to sit?"

Surprised, I nodded and gestured toward my usual booth. I waited for to take her seat before I took mine. She pulled her son out of the stroller and made the sweetest little sounds as he bounced up and down in her lap.

"Motherhood suits you," I told her.

Ryleigh cooed at the baby, before she placed a bottle in

his mouth. "I love being a mother. I never thought it would be like this."

When we were together, Ryleigh had made it a point to say she never wanted kids. I guessed things changed when she fell in love. A waitress came over, poured my coffee and Ryleigh's water, and took our order.

When we were alone again, I asked, "How are you?"

"I'm great," she said. "I'm actually glad I ran into you."

"Really?" I rested my back against the seat. "That's… different."

"The last time we spoke, it was a little tense. It has haunted me since. I guess the shock of seeing that look in your eyes after all this time and hearing you apologize to me was a lot. I was conflicted. I wanted comfort you *and* kick your ass."

I chuckled. "Tell me how you really feel."

"I'm so serious. Over the last several years, I realized that we weren't what I thought we were at the time."

"I think we were pretty good together."

She titled her head. The puzzled look on her face pretty much ensured I wouldn't like what was coming next. "I think there's a bit of revisionist history at play here."

"How so? I didn't imagine the connection, Ry. We had a lot of fun together."

A smile formed on her lips. "Because sex is fun."

"It was more than sex," I argued.

When I walked away, even though it was my dumb decision to leave, I felt gutted for years afterward. That wasn't because we were *just* fucking.

"I thought it could be, too," she murmured. "In hindsight, though, we wouldn't have worked. Obviously, you weren't ready."

"I was a fool."

"But you were an honest fool. Look, if what we had was so damn special, why did you do it?"

"I was a fool," I repeated.

"I don't believe that, Coop. You're one the smartest people I know. I have to believe that some part of you knew that we weren't going anywhere good together."

As much as I hated to admit it, she was probably right. We were both in a new city, hundreds of miles away from home. She was climbing the corporate ladder and I was building something lasting from the bottom up.

"Part of the connection was the convenience," she added. "The familiarity."

One thing that drew me to adult Ryleigh was that she knew me. She'd been there when I was a kid, she'd watched me blow my way through my teenage years, and she'd cried when I moved away. We were like family—save for the intense physical attraction we had to each other.

I dropped my head. Seconds later, I felt her hand on top of mine. "Cooper, when you didn't show up, I was beside myself with anger. But I've come to realize it was more about the *way* you did it, than the fact that you did."

"I'm sorry, Ry," I murmured, flipping my hand over and squeezing hers.

"I forgive you."

Closing my eyes, I let the words wash through me. It felt like a weight had lifted. I'd beat myself up for so long about how I'd handled things between us. "At the time, I didn't know what the hell I was doing. I just knew I never wanted to hurt you."

"We never made any promises. Besides, like I told you, everything is as it should be."

"I do miss you," I confessed. "You are important to me. I want to know about you, what you're doing, what you're planning. I want to know your son."

She smirked. "I have no problem with that. As long as you don't try to touch my booty. Martin will kill your ass."

I barked out a laugh, throwing my hands up. "No touching."

"Promise?"

Nodding, I said, "Promise."

Mama Lil shuffled out of the back with two huge platters of food. "Hey, y'all. I figured I'd do the honors and bring you this delicious cuisine." After she set the plates on the table, she took Ryleigh's now sleeping baby from her arms and disappeared again.

For the next hour, we ate and talked about a little bit of everything from our jobs to the Detroit Pistons' last basketball game.

"Quick question?" She leaned in. "You've successfully diverted this conversation from your future in this town. So, in the spirit of rebuilding friendship, tell me if you've made the decision to move back here."

"You caught that, huh?"

She nodded. "I've known you a long time. Ava told me all about Granddad's wish for you."

I raised a brow. "Did she tell you what color socks I'm wearing?"

"No, but I'm sure they're black."

Laughing, I said, "You're right. They are. And I haven't made my final decision, yet."

With a furrowed brow, she asked, "What are you waiting on?"

The bell above the door to the restaurant jingled, and turned my head just in time to see Angel step into the building. Our eyes locked from across the dining room and she smiled. That wide grin slipped when she noticed I wasn't alone.

"Who is that?" Ryleigh asked.

Even Ryleigh couldn't tear my attention from the woman who'd changed everything in such a short time. I felt the compulsion to explain myself to Angel, assure her that this wasn't what it looked like. It was definitely a new feeling for me.

"Coop?" Ry called.

"Give me a sec," I whispered, before I stood and approached Angel. "Hey."

Angel glanced at Ryleigh, then back at me. "Hi."

"I didn't think you were in town."

The last time we talked, Angel said she wasn't sure she'd be able to come up this weekend, something about a big family dinner.

She swallowed visibly. "I wanted to come see the drywall."

"Ah. I can take you by the house now, if you want."

Angel retreated back a step. "If you had other plans… I don't want to intrude."

Unable to stop myself from touching her, I squeezed her hand. "You're not. Come on." I led her over to the table, where Ryleigh was watching me intently. "Angel, this is Ryleigh."

Angel smiled and waved. "Hi."

"Hey!" Ryleigh stood and dropped her napkin onto the table. "Nice to meet you."

"Same," Angel said.

"Do you live in Rosewood Heights?" Ryleigh asked.

Angel looked at me for a split second, then answered, "Not yet. Cooper is working on my aunt's house."

Ryleigh's eyes widened, and I knew she was putting the pieces together. We'd talked about the Fox house, but I hadn't mentioned anything specifically about Angel. "Ah. So your aunt was Ms. Fox?" She gave Angel her condolences. "I'm so sorry for your loss."

Angel thanked her. "Cooper and his team have done an amazing job so far. My aunt would've been so happy with it."

They segued into a short discussion about the house, while I tried to figure out why I couldn't seem to add anything to the conversation. It seemed surreal to see Ryleigh and Angel talking. Now, they were complimenting each other's clothes.

"I'm sorry to interrupt your breakfast," Angel said.

"Girl," Ry waved a dismissive hand. "You didn't. I was actually getting ready to grab my baby and Mama Lil and get up out of here."

As if on cue, Mama Lil emerged from the back of the restaurant, baby in tow. She walked over to them. "Hi, Angel. Hungry?"

"I was going to place a carryout order," Angel told her.

Mama Lil set the still sleeping baby back in the stroller. "Okay. I'll take your order, sweetie."

Angel stepped over to the register with Mama Lil. Once she was out of earshot, Ryleigh said, "I think I have my answer now."

I shot her a sidelong glance. "You *think* you have your answer."

Ryleigh moved closer. "It's pretty clear to me. You're smitten."

I peered down at Ryleigh. "When did you turn into Ava?"

She giggled, shoving me playfully. "Now, you know better. I love my friend, but I'm definitely not her."

"I know."

"Seriously, though. She's beautiful." She poked me in my shoulder. "You better not fuck this up."

It was my turn to laugh now. "Go home, Ry."

Angel and Mama Lil made their way back over a few

minutes later. After a long awkward silence, Mama Lil announced, "I'm tired, Ry. Let's go."

"Thanks again, Mama Lil," Angel said.

The older woman waved her hand towel. "Chile, that's what we're here for."

Ryleigh slid her coat on. "Alright. Mama Lil, let's go." She gave me a hug and whispered, "Remember what I said, sir. No fuck ups allowed."

After they exchanged goodbyes with Angel, they left.

"She's nice."

"We grew up together," I explained. "She's one of Ava's best friends."

Angel nodded. "And who is she to you?"

Chapter 7

ANGEL

Driving to Rosewood Heights on a whim, leaving Mehki with my parents, to see Cooper was a huge step for me. Hoping that we'd be able to spend some time together without Mehki had fueled my decision because I felt time alone time was needed in order to move forward. Taking a chance that he would agree with me was a risk. And realizing he wasn't sitting alone thinking about me, but having breakfast with a beautiful, nice woman sucked. I knew I shouldn't be angry, but I was pissed. At myself. For letting my heart skip ahead of my brain.

I'd asked him a question. But for whatever reason I didn't have an answer. The only thing I had was an apology when he had to go home to handle an important *and* unexpected business call.

Now I was sitting outside on the balcony of my rental, wondering where I went wrong and why I was still here.

Instead of taking my ass back to Charleston, I'd settled in to wait for him. Because he told me he'd come back so we could talk.

I poured my second glass of wine and dialed Tee.

My friend's face popped up on the screen a second later. "What's up, boo?"

"Tell me again why you encouraged me to come back here?" I took a sip of wine. "If I was coming back to be alone, I could have done that in Charleston."

"Girl, he said he was coming back." Tee walked through her house and plopped down on her bed. "Give him some time."

"Time to what? Make me feel like a bigger fool."

"You're overreacting. Right now, we don't even know who the woman was to him."

I'd explained everything to Tee when he'd left earlier, complete with a full description of Ryleigh. "You didn't see how he looked at her. I swear, they used to fuck."

Tee's mouth fell open. "Sis! Stop. Again, you don't know that. Don't jump to conclusions."

"She had a baby. What if it's his?"

Sighing, Tee said, "Don't you think he would've told you if he had a kid by now? In fact, didn't you say he told you he didn't?"

Tee was right. They'd talked about kids when he'd mentioned he'd been married once. None of his brothers had children. Only his sister did. I knew that. "Fine," I grumbled. "It just didn't feel right. My gut is telling me—"

"That isn't your gut. That's your inability to let yourself be happy."

I clamped my mouth shut. "I'm hanging up."

"Bye. But don't call me back and complain about anything else."

Of course, I didn't hang up. I just sat there, staring at

my friend and finishing my wine. When I was done, I set the glass down. "Tee, I'm scared."

Her eyes softened. "I know. But if you stay scared, you'll never do anything different. You know this."

"I—" The doorbell chimed and I sat up straight. "It's him."

"Or it could be a killer," Tee suggested.

I glared at her. "I'm going to answer the door."

"Can you just do me a favor and put some something on those lips?"

I laughed. "Bye." I ended the video chat and rushed to the bathroom, put my lip gloss on, and brushed my hair back into a tamer version of a pony-tail. On my way to the door, I picked up my coat and hung it up. Taking a quick, calming breath, I opened the door.

Cooper smiled. "Hello."

I stepped aside and gestured for him to come in. Without a word, I walked over to the sofa and plopped down on it, pulling one of the throw pillows on top of my lap.

He slid out of his boots, and joined me a few seconds later. "I'm sorry."

"Is everything okay?" I asked.

"Yeah." He rubbed the back of his neck. "Crisis averted."

I squeezed the pillow. "Good."

He reached out and ran a finger over my mouth. I could hear my breath hitch and wondered if he'd heard it, too. It was so loud. "I'm happy you're here."

"Are you?"

Cooper nodded. "I am." He pulled me closer to him. "You asked me a question earlier."

Distracted by his thumb moving in circles on my knee,

his scent wafting to my nose, his breath on my lips, I nodded.

"Ryleigh and I are friends."

"Only friends?" I managed to say.

"Yes. But it wasn't always that way. We had a thing years ago. It ended in a not so good way, which I always regretted."

"You hurt her?"

"I did," he confessed. "We didn't talk for a long time—until the funeral."

The fact that he'd chosen honesty lifted some of the doubt that had crept in earlier. I was grateful he didn't lie. I knew what I saw.

"We'd been so much to each other over the years that I had to make it right," he continued. "Ya know?"

I swallowed hard. "Yes. I get it."

"I've done a lot of dirt, Angel."

I caressed his face. "Cooper, we don't have to do this. I don't expect you to be perfect, to never have done anything wrong."

He held my hands against his cheeks. "I want to be upfront with you."

"Yeah, but you don't have to tell me everything tonight."

Barking out a laugh, he brushed his lips against each of my palms. "Angel," he murmured against my skin. "This is different for me."

"How so?"

"In the past, I've never stayed around long enough to have this conversation."

"Not even with Ryleigh?" I asked.

"She was… With her it was easier because we had a shared past, a common history. We knew each other. I didn't have to explain my fucked up relationship with my father. I didn't have to pretend to be something I'm not."

"Do you still love her?" I held my breath, awaiting his answer.

His eyes flashed to mine. "For a while, I considered her the woman who got away."

If she is the one who got away, who am I? "You wanted her back?"

"I told myself that if she ever gave me another chance, I would take it."

I lifted a brow. "Really?"

"She gave me a reality check." He laughed softly. "Made me realize some things that I hadn't thought of. Long story short, what we had wasn't what I thought it was—and it's over."

I let out a slow breath. He'd been so forthright, I felt wrong for not sharing more of my past with him. He knew Mehki's father was dead, but that's really it. "Malachi died before Mehki was born," I said. "We were high school sweethearts. He was the only man that I've ever loved." I paused, waiting for Cooper to say something. When he didn't, I continued, "The night he died, I didn't think I'd make it. But I did because I knew that I had someone who I needed me and I wanted to be there for him."

"Mehki is lucky to have you," he said.

"He definitely keeps me on my toes."

"You came here without him."

"To see you," I admitted. "I haven't kissed a man in almost seven years. I needed to talk about it."

His eyes widened. "Seriously?"

I nodded. "I've lived for Mehki, only for him."

"And you want to talk about the kiss?"

"Don't you think we should?"

He shook his head, his gaze dropping to my mouth.

Leaning closer, he whispered, "I think we shouldn't over-think it anymore."

I brushed my lips against his. "I think I agree with—" Before I could finish my sentence, he pulled me to him and into a searing kiss.

Breaking apart, he rested his forehead against mine. "Angel."

I opened my eyes. "Huh?"

"I'm still tempted." He nipped my chin.

"Good."

He kissed me again, drawing a low moan from me. My head hit the cushions of the couch and he settled on top of me, kissing me, biting me. Every lick, every touch, every groan cracked me open a little more. He made me feel a little crazy and a lot horny.

I tugged his shirt off and finally got my feel of the bare skin of his back, of his stomach. He felt good, hard and hot everywhere. His erection against my core made me want to rip off his pants so he could get closer, to ease the ache that took over my body.

"Angel," he whispered, sucking my bottom lip in his mouth. "We're at the point of no return, baby."

I groaned. I thought the way he said my name was sexy as fuck, but the way he called me baby? *Shit.* I was on fire, and only he could douse the flames. "Cooper," I bit out. "Don't stop."

His head popped up, his eyes boring into mine. A slight frown creased his brow. "Are you sure?"

I thought about it for a second, before nodding. "I think so."

Cooper arched a brow. "You *think*?"

His question gave me pause. Then, again, reality shined a bright light in my face. *Why can't I let myself be great? And satisfied?* I sighed heavily and sat up. Running my fingers over my hair, I turned to Cooper. "I'm sorry."

He pulled me against him. "No need to be sorry. I'd rather stop now than do something you'll regret later."

I burrowed into his side. "I bet you've never had to deal with this before."

"No, but it's okay." He tipped my chin up and kissed me. "I'll wait."

I wrapped my arms around him, enjoying being so near to him. "Thank you." A few minutes later, my stomach growled. I felt the rumble of his laughter against me. Peering up at him, I said, "I had a lot of wine. On an empty stomach."

"You didn't eat dinner?"

I tossed him an exaggerated pout and shook my head. "I'm hungry."

He tapped my nose. "You sound like Mehki."

Giggling, I shoved him away playfully. "He is his mother's child."

Cooper stood, pulling me to my feet. "Well, I guess I'll feed you."

That night we had Chinese, watched a movie, and fell asleep on the sofa in each other's arms. And it was perfect. *He* was perfect

---

I AWAKENED THE NEXT MORNING, wrapped in Cooper's arms. It had been years since I'd slept in someone's arms. It had been too long since I'd felt safe, free enough to let myself *be* with someone. I *needed* more. And even though I'd put the brakes on going further yesterday, I was *ready* today. But this wasn't a movie, morning breath was a real thing, and I needed a shower. Placing a kiss on his cheek, I slipped off the couch.

After my shower, I spent more than a normal amount of time trying to find something to wear that didn't consist of frumpy shirts or motherly shorts. When I realized I didn't own anything sexy. I said fuck it and pulled out a pair of yoga capris and a tank.

Several minutes later, I was in the kitchen cooking. The bacon was in the oven and the pancakes were bubbling on the griddle when I heard him stir.

"Good morning," he said, his voice raspy.

I flipped the pancakes. "Morning." Glancing at him out of the corner of my eye as he approached, I said, "Hungry?"

"I could eat. Especially if you're making pancakes."

I smirked. "I figured I'd blow your mind with my buttermilk batter."

He chuckled. "Sounds like my kind of morning." He slid onto one of the stools at the breakfast bar. "Do you have any plans today?"

I slid the pancakes onto the platter and poured another round of mix onto the griddle. "No. I'm all—" I stopped myself from saying *yours*, because I realized I had no idea if he even wanted to spend the entire day with me. "I'm going to chill around here today."

"Do you want to give me your time today?"

I closed my eyes relieved that he said what I'd hoped he would say. "Sure. What do you want to do?"

I hope he wants to do me. He'd been such a gentleman, letting me control the pace. And maybe this made me a little wishy washy, but now I wanted him to take the lead.

"First… do you have an extra toothbrush?" he asked.

I pulled the bacon from the oven, smiling to myself. "I

already laid a towel and a toothbrush out for you. If you want to take a shower, you can use the master bathroom."

"Thanks, baby." He disappeared down the hallway, leaving me to my wayward thoughts.

I took a deep breath, pressing my palm against my stomach. My body seemed to have a mind of its own, already jumping ahead to the main event. I sensed, though, that he wanted to take his time with me, so I had to resolve myself to not getting some this morning. Maybe later. *Hopefully* later.

When he returned, before he could take his seat again, I whirled around. "Can I be honest?"

His brows drew close together. "Haven't you always?"

"I have," I said, nodding rapidly. "But… I haven't done this in really long time."

"What? Cook pancakes?"

I slid his plate over to him. "I do that all of the time. Mehki loves them."

He picked up a piece of bacon. "So he told me."

"I want you," I blurted out.

He paused, mouth open, bacon in the air. He set it back down on his plate. "Um… I know?"

Bracing my elbows against the counter, I peered up at him. "This is probably going to sound weird, but I guess I've never actually *dated* anyone? I mean, Malachi and I… Things just pretty much happened between us. One minute we were playing basketball outside and the next minute we were going to Homecoming. Then, we were together."

I never had any doubts that Malachi loved me, because he'd cherished me, took care of me. As spontaneous as he tried to be, he wasn't *that* guy. He was reserved, he liked order, routine. I knew what to expect with him, because we were alike in that way. And Cooper was so different, so free, so… *un*reserved.

At the same time, there were many things they had in common with each other. They both worked in construction, they both owned a business, they both loved kids, they both had large families. But Cooper… I didn't know anyone like him. He made me laugh until I cried and he didn't take himself too seriously. He wasn't afraid to admit that he'd fucked up a lot. He didn't bother to hide the shadows behind his eyes. And that only made me want him even more.

"Angel," Cooper said, pulling me from my thoughts. "I think where you're having trouble is you're a planner. You're methodical. You're used to doing things in a certain way and you kind of panic when you can't have your hand on everything."

"That's exactly right."

"Can you come over here?" I rounded the breakfast bar and stopped in front of him. He gripped my hips, pulled me closer, and kissed me. "Is it too much to ask that you let me take the reins today?"

Digging my nails into his thighs, I said, "No."

"I need you dressed and ready to go in the next hour." Then, he picked up his piece of bacon and bit into it. Out of the corner of his eye, he watched me, standing there, staring at him. "You might want to go handle your business."

Blinking, I backed away bumping into the other barstool and nearly tumbling to the ground. "I'm just… Okay, I'll…" I stammered. "I'll go handle that." I hurried down the hall and did as I was told.

After hours of jampacked action, we arrived back to my rental. Cooper was true to his word and handled every aspect of the day. We golfed, ate lunch on the beach, saw the movie I'd been wanting to see, had hibachi for dinner. Everything about today had been beautiful. My impromptu visit had turned out to be more than I'd hoped for.

I plopped down on the sofa. "That food was so good."

He sat down next to me, shoulder to shoulder. "How have you never eaten sushi before today?"

I turned my head to face him. "I just didn't think I'd like it."

Cooper lifted my legs into his lap, and took off my shoes. "Now you know you do."

"Oh God," I moaned when he started massaging my foot. "You're good at this. Thank you." We'd walked so much today that my feet started hurting sometime after lunch.

He flashed a wicked smirk my way, pressing his thumb into the arch of my foot. "I'm good at a lot of shit."

I sat up and gripped his collar, tugging him closer. "Don't start something you can't finish."

He pulled off my socks, then glanced over at me, his gaze raking over every inch of my body. The heat in his eyes was unmistakable, and it called to me on a primal level. "All I need is permission."

My heart… It was beating out of control, fast and loud in my ears as I considered his words. I craved this man, I wanted him to have his way with me. Shivering, I licked my lips and let out a slow breath. "Permission granted."

His fingers grazed over my ankles and inched up my legs. He stopped at the button of my jeans and flicked it with his thumb. He unzipped my jeans slowly, like he was unwrapping a gift on Christmas. My body was now screaming at me to scream at him to go faster, to ease the ache that had settled between my thighs. I'd promised to let him take the reins today, so I would wait it out. But, damn if I didn't want to mount him and fuck him until I got the release I wanted.

He peeled my jeans off and tossed them behind him. Then he kissed from the tops of my feet all the way up to my navel. Without a word, he ripped my panties off. *Oh shit.* I gripped the cushion of the couch. At this point, I didn't even think I needed the sex to come. I was so ready, so on the edge, I knew it wouldn't take long.

Then, his tongue… *Oh damn.* The moment his wicked tongue touched my clit, I was done. I came so hard and fast I couldn't breathe. When the trembling subsided, I opened my eyes to find him staring at me, a cute ass smirk on his lips.

"Don't say anything," I said, trying to catch my breath. "It's been a long time."

He laughed, while he unbuttoned my shirt. "No worries. You got about three, maybe four more of those coming before I'm done with you."

Oh.

Cooper must have kissed every inch of my body, igniting every nerve ending I had, by the time he pressed his lips to mine. I was so caught up in him, I couldn't think or feel or smell or see anything but him.

He only broke the kiss to breathe—and to take his shirt off. He rested against me, kissed my cheeks and my chin, before sinking his teeth into the base of my neck. "Angel," he murmured, soothing the same spot with his tongue and his mouth. "You have tempted me at every turn. I want you..." He rested his forehead against the space between my breasts.

When his gaze met mine again, I sucked in a deep breath. *I'm so in trouble.* Good trouble. And I wanted it. "Cooper." My voice sounded strange to my own ears.

"…In a way I've never wanted anyone else." He sucked

a nipple into his mouth. His low groan was just as effective as his hands and his mouth. I arched into him, wordlessly begging him to pick up the pace. His hand cupped my core and he slipped one finger—then two—inside. Pressing his thumb against my clit. "Number two."

I gasped for air as another orgasm shot through me. Once again, he waited until I opened my eyes, to kiss me. This time, I took back some of the control, unbuttoned his jeans, and pushed them off. His boxer briefs followed shortly after.

I stroked him, enjoying the feel of him in my palm, his low hiss against my skin. He bent over and grabbed a condom out of his pocket. He handed it to me, and I snatched it from him and slid it on. A beat later, he was pressed against me, his dick against my pussy. With our gazes locked on each other, he entered me.

He closed his eyes, waited a moment, then he started to move. Slowly at first, almost too slow. It didn't take long for us to find our rhythm, and the pace picked up. The race to completion was frenzied, mouths fused together, eyes open, hands moving. When orgasm number three snuck up on me, I clung to him, letting the waves of pleasure take over. Cooper joined me seconds later, groaning out my name.

We didn't move for what seemed like forever. I didn't want to let him go. Ever. But soon enough, he lifted his head, his hooded eyes boring into mine. "Give me ten minutes, and then you can get number four."

Chapter 8

COOPER

"Mr. Cooper, am I doing it right?"

I eyed the line of blue paint Mehki had just rolled onto the wall. We'd been at it for thirty minutes. Lil Man wanted a step-by-step instruction before he would even dip the roller into the paint. "Looks good to me." I gave him a high five. "Make sure the lines are straight."

Mehki nodded. "Okay."

Construction was almost complete. The painters were spread out over the house, moving through each room efficiently. But this room, which would soon be Mehki's, would be last because I promised him I would teach him how to paint.

"Wow," Angel said, entering the newly renovated space. "Looks so bright in here."

She stepped over to us and brushed the top of Mehki's head. Bending low, she let Mehki tell her all about our process. Angel, the woman, was already a site to behold. But Angel, the mother? Every time I saw her with her son, I felt my heart squeeze in my chest. She was perfection.

It had been a couple of weeks since we'd had a weekend alone, but that hadn't stopped me from taking advantage of every private moment between us. I couldn't get enough of her, the way she smelled, the sound of her laughter, the feel of her skin against mine. Those hips, her legs, her face. Every part of her seemed made especially for me. I wanted to conquer her, stake my claim, mount my flag. But the closer we got to the completion date, the more I feared all of it would vanish. That the bubble around us would pop.

I still hadn't made the decision to work at Prescott Holdings, but I had continued to make inroads with my father. I'd even attended several company meetings, telling myself that it was just to study the lay of the land—in case I decided to stay.

Prescott-Hayes had thrived under Preston's day-to-day leadership, and I had no doubt he didn't really need me in Detroit on a full-time basis. But still… *Can I walk away from it? From her?*

Yet, it wasn't just her I'd be walking away from if I decided to go back to Detroit. The boy standing next to me, his brow furrowed in concentration, had worked his way into my heart. He reminded me of myself at that age, always inquisitive, always questioning. He deserved to be happy. But did I deserve him?

"Cooper?" Angel called. She stepped into me, bumping her hip against me. "You good?"

My gaze dropped to Mehki. His short height prevented him from completing his lines, so I'd gone behind him finishing each row of paint as he made his way down the wall. I topped off his line, and glanced back at Angel. "Yeah, I'm good."

She eyed me skeptically. "Sure?"

I reached out to touch her, but she dodged me. It was typical for her to avoid any prolonged displays of affection in front of Mehki. I understood it. After all, she was his mother, she protected him fiercely, and we hadn't made any promises to each other. We both agreed to just see where things would lead.

"See, Mommie!"

Grinning, Angel said, "You're doing such a good job, babe."

"Mr. Cooper told me to go slow, so I'm going slow." He turned his attention back to the wall. "I have to be careful."

Covering her smile, she said, "Okay, son. You got this." She met my gaze and murmured, "At this rate, you'll be done by September."

I snorted. "We'll be done tomorrow. The real painters will take over very soon."

She folded her arms across her chest. "Good."

Holding out my roller to her, I asked, "Want to give it a try?"

"Nope," she chirped.

"Hello?" I recognized the voice immediately, coming from downstairs.

"We have company," Mehki said, running out of the room.

"Don't run!" she shouted after him. A cute crease formed on her brow and I brushed a thumb over forehead. "Who is it?"

I grabbed her hand and squeezed. "Come on. I want you to meet somebody."

Dallas was standing at the base of the staircase, talking to Mehki. When she spotted me, she smiled. "Hey, punk."

Shaking my head, I said, "What's up?" I gave her a hug.

"Since you refuse to answer your phone, I figured I'd surprise your black a—" Dallas scratched the back of her neck, peering down at Mehki. "Behind."

I introduced Dallas to Angel and Mehki. They greeted each other with smiles and handshakes. "Dallas is a good friend," I explained.

"If I'm such a good friend, why did you leave me alone with Preston's ass?" She sighed. She apologized to Angel. "Apparently, I can't seem to cut off the cuss words."

"Mommie says shit all the time," Mehki said with a shrug. "And damn."

Dallas and I cracked up.

"Mehki!" Angel covered his mouth. "He's so… He doesn't forget anything."

"A man after my own heart." Dallas gave Mehki a fist bump. Turning to me, she said, "I was in Charleston on business. Thought I'd run up on you, see what you been doing."

"Want to grab something to eat?" I suggested.

"Sure," they all said simultaneously.

Later on, we were all seated at a booth in The Divine Café. "Can you stop telling all my business?" I warned Dallas. "We have little ears around."

"That's why he has on his earbuds," Angel said, prodding Dallas to continue.

"This fool gets married anyway, after I warned him to stay away from that woman. Then begs me to get him out of it—two days later."

Angel looked at me, her mouth open. "Wow, Cooper."

I'd told her about my marriage, but I'd left out a lot of

the details like the length and the circumstances. Shrugging, I said, "We all know I've fucked up from time to time."

Angel sipped on her sweet tea. "So you're a marriage broker?" she asked Dallas.

Dallas popped a french fry in her mouth and nodded. "Sometimes marrying for love isn't an option. And if you do love someone, you might not want to just give away all of your worldly possessions if it doesn't work out."

The two woman had hit it off, much like Angel and Ryleigh did. Which was surprising because Dallas didn't really get along with new people. She kept her circle tight.

"That's so interesting," Angel said. "I thought about law school for a while. In the end, I went with the MBA because I liked finance better."

"And I *hate* finance," Dallas grumbled. "At least when it doesn't involve settlements."

Mehki hopped up. "I have to use the bathroom."

Angel stood. "I'll be right back." She grabbed his hand and left.

Dallas grinned. "I like her."

Eyeing her, I asked, "What else?"

Shrugging, she said, "Nothing else. She's smart, intelligent… I love Mehki. He's a trip."

"I…" *Love them both* died on my lips. It was way too soon for that. *Right*?

Dallas arched a brow. "You like them, too."

"Of course, I like them. I've spent a lot of time with them."

"More than just *time*. You're sleeping with her, right?"

I glanced at the hallway to make sure Angel was nowhere near this discussion. "Damn, man. You just put it out there like that."

"It's pretty obvious."

"Just because I told you about Ryleigh doesn't mean I'm about to tell you about Angel."

Despite what anyone might have believed, Dallas and I didn't really talk much about our relationships or sex. I knew she was fucking and she knew I was, too. The Ryleigh conversation was a fluke, a one-off. And she only knew about Jacqueline because I needed her professional services—before *and* after the wedding.

"Coop, we're friends. We should be able to have an adult conversation. Not *too* adult," she added. "By the way, Ryleigh mentioned she had one with you."

I glared at her. "And I'm sure she told you it was none of your business."

Dallas nodded. "She did. But that's beside the point." She planted her palms on the table. "I just… she has a kid, Coop. The rules are different."

"I know that," I groaned. "I'm not a fuckin' idiot."

She threw her hands up in surrender. "Just sayin'. Tread carefully."

Dallas hadn't said anything wrong. Angel and Mehki were a package deal and I wouldn't want to hurt either of them. "I got it."

"And if you pull one of your asshole moves, I *will* cut you." She finished her drink. "This is damn good tea. I need you to bring some of this shit home with you."

Angel and Mehki rejoined us. I looked at Mehki, who was clinging to her. She smiled, but it didn't reach her eyes. "Mehki's not feeling too well."

I stood. "What's wrong?"

She shrugged. "Stomachache."

"I'll take you home." I paid the bill and we left. Instead of going back to the Fox house, I took them to Angel's Airbnb first. Inside, she told Mehki to go lay down and she'd be there in a few minutes. I brushed a piece of hair from her forehead. "I'll be back."

"You don't have to," Angel said. "I know you want to spend time with your friend."

"*Just* friends," I assured her.

She smiled. Again, it seemed forced. "I know."

I kissed her. "I'll see you in a little while."

The drive to Dallas' car was silent. My mind was racing, wondering what was wrong with Angel, how Mehki was feeling. I hated leaving them even for this short time. I wanted to be able to comfort Lil Man. I wanted to help Angel take care of him. I wondered if Angel would let me help her. *Forever.*

When we finally arrived at the Fox house, Dallas said. "I have an early flight. I better hit the road." She got out of the car, and I followed her to the rental. I opened her door, but she didn't get in. Instead, she turned to me. "I think I was wrong."

I gave her sidelong glance. "About?"

"Back when I said you liked them," she explained. "I think it's more than that."

I stared her, swallowing hard. Because I knew that it *was* more than me simply liking them. Somewhere along the line, I started wanting mornings with them, eating breakfast together, taking Mehki to basketball games, teaching him everything I knew. Seeing them on the weekends wasn't enough. I wanted to see them every day, I wanted to go to bed and know that they'd be there when I woke up.

"Maybe," I admitted.

"If your feelings for her are what I think they are, I hope you can let yourself tell her."

"Don't you think it's too soon?"

"My parents fell in love in a week. And they still think

the sun rises and sets with each other. So anything is possible."

Dallas wasn't the type to wax poetic about love and possibilities. But it was nice to be able to hear her perspective. "What if I…?"

"Fuck up? You will. That's normal. And it's okay." She sighed. "I love you, Coop."

"Are you sick or something?"

She threw her head back and laughed. "No, fool." She smacked my shoulder. "I'm just rooting for you."

"You know I love you, too."

Nodding, she said, "I do. Just so you know, I cannot be held liable for what I do to Preston when you're no longer the buffer."

I chuckled. "Leave the man alone. I don't know why y'all keep hanging out if you can't get along."

"I feel sorry for his dopey ass."

"Right."

"I'm so serious. He needs help. I can't wait until he finds a woman." She slid into car. "Bye, Coop. Answer your damn phone next time I call."

"Maybe. Bye, Dallas." I closed her door and waited until she drove off before I left.

"MR. COOPER?"

I looked down at Mehki, who was cuddled up next to me. Instead of asking me to read him a story, he'd asked me to explain to him why I thought Spider-Man wasn't the greatest Avenger. The six-year-old had already made up his mind, so he had an argument ready for every point I attempted to make. In the end, we agreed to disagree.

"Yeah, Lil Man?"

"When we move into our house, are you still going to come see us?"

I peered into his innocent brown eyes. The question caught me off guard. I didn't want to tell him yes, and I couldn't tell him no. "Do you want me to come see you?" I asked.

He nodded. "Yes. I would miss you if you didn't come see me. I want you to marry my Mommie so I can have a Daddy. When I grow up, I want to build houses like you."

My throat closed up. Clearing it, I said, "Really?" Having a legacy, someone to take over *my* business was a dream I didn't know I had before now.

"Yes. And I hope my hands get as big as yours so I can shuffle cards like you do."

I laughed, remembering our game of Uno last night. "You'll get there soon enough."

"Mommie smiles when you're here. She sings more. Not just lullabies but love songs."

Mehki was killing me, systematically taking me apart with his words. He was so sincere, so honest, I couldn't lie to him. "I'm happy when your mom is here, too." On my birthday last month, she'd called me and sang Happy Birthday on my voicemail. I lost count of the amount of times I'd listened to the recording. "And I'm glad she's singing."

Angel had confessed that she loved to sing, but for so long she didn't have anything to sing about.

"She's good," he said.

She's my Angel. "I agree."

"Mr. Cooper?"

"Yes, Lil Man?"

"I love you."

Closing my eyes, I let out a slow breath. "I love you, too. And you don't have to worry about what happens when you move into the house. I'm always going to be here for you if you need me."

"Alright, boys." Angel ventured into the room. "Time for this little one to get some sleep."

I slid off the bed and watched her tuck Mehki in. Once she finished, we walked out into the living room.

"He was so sad we couldn't finish the game of Monopoly we started last night," she said.

"He mentioned it the moment I got here." The board was still set up on the kitchen table. But Lil Man fell asleep right before he landed on Boardwalk and had to give me all of his money. "Maybe we can finish tomorrow."

Angel eyed me. "Did Dallas make it back to Charleston?"

"She texted me about twenty minutes ago from her hotel room."

"Good. She's so funny."

I chuckled. "She's really not."

"Well, she cracked me up." She sat down on the couch, tucking her feet under her. I walked over to her and pulled her to her feet. "What are you doing?"

So far, we'd never made love while Mehki was in the house, but I needed her. Cradling her face in my palms, I pulled her into a kiss. She wrapped her arms around my shoulders, leaning into me and letting me set the pace. We kissed all the way to her bedroom. Once inside, I closed *and* locked the door.

"Cooper?" she whispered, trying to put some space between us.

I hooked my finger into the waistband of her jeans and tugged her to me. "I'm asking for permission." I'd said the same thing to her the first time we were together, but this time the question wasn't simple. The answer wasn't either, because I wasn't asking for just one night, or even asking for permission to touch her. I wanted *every* night, I wanted her to let me love her. Because I did. I loved her so much.

Angel searched my eyes, like she was looking for something in mine that she couldn't see. "Cooper, I..."

"What is it?"

She stared at me a moment longer. Then, she kissed me, sucking my bottom lip into her mouth. "Nothing," she murmured. "Permission granted."

I scooped her into my arms and carried her over to the bed. Laying her down, I stripped her naked and removed my clothes in short order. Standing above her, I took her in, raking my gaze over every part of her. She was so beautiful, so amazing. I wanted to take my time with her tonight, worship her, cherish every minute she let me be with her like this.

In a few short months, she'd changed my world. And now I couldn't imagine my life without her and Mehki. And since the words were seemingly lodged in my throat, I wanted to show her how much she meant to me.

Climbing onto the bed, I kissed my way up her body, stopping to pay special attention to her clit, sucking it into my mouth before she came, with my name on her lips. I continued my trek up, dipping my tongue in her belly button then tugging at her nipple with my teeth, before I sucked it into my mouth.

Her fingernails dug in my shoulders as I brushed my lips across her collarbone, over her jawline, up to her ear. "*My* Angel," I murmured against her ear.

She purred. "Coop, please."

I loved when she begged for me. Because I wanted to give her everything she desired. I hurried with the condom, sheathing myself and pressing my dick against her entrance. Slowly, I thrust into her enjoying the way we fit together.

I squeezed my eyes shut, willing myself not to come before she did. But she felt so good, so tight, so *mine*. It was a strange feeling realizing that someone had the power to destroy me. But I knew *she* could. At the same time, I wasn't willing to walk away from this.

I moved slow, wanting to drag this out for hours. But the need for completion made that feel impossible. Gripping her hips, I pushed in deeper with each thrust until she was begging me to let her come, to let her fly. We came together, with my heart pounding so hard in my chest, it seemed to shatter me, crack me open.

After a moment, I opened my eyes to find her staring at me, tears in her eyes. I kissed her cheeks, then brushed my mouth over hers.

"Baby?" she whispered, running her finger over my cheek. "Thank you."

Frowning I peered into her eyes. "Why are you thanking me?" The comment seemed strange in the moment, and I wanted to fire off a barrage of questions to get to the bottom of it.

"For everything," she said. "Meeting you was a game changer for me. I'll always remember the time we spent together fondly."

Her words seemed… final. Like she planned on going away or something. And another feeling started to build in my gut—a bad feeling. But before I could ask her another question, she placed her finger over my lips.

"Don't," she said. "Just… hold me."

I rolled onto my back, pulling her into my arms. Kissing her brow, I said, "I won't let go."

A few minutes later, I heard her soft snores. "I love you," I whispered to her sleeping form.

Chapter 9

COOPER

"Welcome home, Ms. Crawford."

Angel grinned, stepping onto the porch of her now complete home. "I can't believe it's done!"

We'd finished two weeks ahead of schedule, and when I called Angel to let her know the good news, she hopped on the road and drove straight to Rosewood Heights. "All done," I confirmed. "Appliances, flooring… everything."

She hugged me. "You're my hero."

It had been weeks since I'd seen her. One weekend, she'd called and said she was flying to L.A. with Tee to look for houses. The second weekend was Mother's Day, so she'd stayed in Charleston to celebrate the holiday with her family.

I leaned down, placing a kiss to her mouth. "I missed you."

She smiled. "I missed you, too."

“Where’s Mehki? I have a surprise for him.”

Averting her gaze, she walked over to the new front door. “I left him with Tee.” She ran her hand over the intricate details in the glass. “I love this.”

“I figured you would.”

She glanced at me over her shoulder. “You going to show me around?”

Nodding, I motioned for her to step inside, then followed her in. “Oh my God! Cooper! I love it.”

We’d managed to salvage a lot of the original features, but Angel liked a more modern design so we added a lot of contemporary elements. “I figured you’d love the grey.”

“I do.” She spun around in the living room, pointing out little details. “Everything looks so much brighter in here. No more dark paneling and wallpaper.”

We started at the sunroom, to the kitchen, then upstairs. Grabbing her hand, I led her into Mehki’s room first.

She placed her hand over her mouth. “Oh, Cooper, you bought him a bed?”

I walked over to the full-over-full bunk bed. “This more than a bed. It’s a fort.” I’d even purchased the bedding. Spider-Man everything.

“He’s going to be so excited.” Her voice cracked and I frowned.

That gnawing feeling of dread crept back into my gut. “Are you okay, baby?”

She nodded. “I’m just so… happy.” She rounded the bed, screaming and jumping back when she spotted my other surprise. “Cooper, I’m going to kill you. You bought him a damn tarantula.”

“You said you were leaning toward a yes,” I explained. “So, I called a friend of mine and made it happen. If you want me to take it back, I will.”

She sent me a mock glare. “No. He’s going to need something to keep him busy this summer.”

We headed to the next room. After we’d seen everything else on the second floor, I led her into the master bedroom. An air mattress was blown up in the middle of the room.

“You trying to tell me something?” she asked saucily.

“Maybe,” I said.

Angel smirked, then disappeared into the master bathroom. I heard her gasp and knew she’d spotted my surprise for her. I entered the room. She was sitting in her Aunt Lou’s original clawfoot tub. “You really outdid yourself,” she said.

Back in January, I wasn’t sure we’d be able to save the tub, but I found someone who was able to restore it. The hell I went through making it happen was worth the smile on her face now, though.

“I can’t wait to soak in it.” She closed her eyes. “Have a nice bubble bath. Candles, music. Me time.”

Dropping to my knees, I kissed her. “You deserve it.”

She traced my jawline with her finger. “You’re amazing, Cooper. I’m so grateful for the work you’ve done. Aunt Lou would’ve been ecstatic.”

“I didn’t bring her things back because I wasn’t sure what stuff you were going to keep. But I’ve already reserved the movers when you’re ready.”

“I ordered new furniture for most of the rooms already. I had planned to take Mehki shopping for his bedroom set, but you saved me a trip to the store.”

“I wanted to do something nice for you both.”

My phone buzzed. I pulled it out of my pocket and glanced at the screen. It was Preston. Standing, I answered, “What’s up?”

I left the bathroom as Preston gave me an update on a

new bid we'd put in with the City of Detroit. "Good news," I said. "I should be able to come back in a week or two."

"If you can't be here, we have everything handled," Preston told me.

"Nah, I want to be there for the initial planning meetings," I insisted. "This is huge for us."

"Are you at the Fox house?" he asked.

"I am. Just showed Angel around."

Preston had flown down last week to help me put the final touches on everything. While he was here, we had a few beers and a deep conversation. I told him about Angel and Mehki, and my desire to have a more permanent place in their life.

"Did she love it?" he asked.

"Why don't you ask her yourself?" I touched the camera button and his face appeared on the screen. Walking back into the bathroom, I told Angel, "Someone has a question for you." I handed her the phone.

"Hi Preston," she said.

Angel and Mehki had met Preston a few months ago when he presented his design to her in person. As with everyone in my life, including my parents, my brothers, Dallas, and Ryleigh, she'd endeared herself to him rather quickly.

"Well?" Preston asked.

Smiling widely, she said, "I love it. I'm sitting in the tub now, envisioning the near future when Mehki and I can settle in."

"I'm glad. Next time I come down there, I expect you to make me some of those pancakes Coop is always raving about."

I shrugged when she glanced over at me. "I can't help it," I said. "You know I love them."

She giggled. "Okay, Preston. I got you."

They talked for a few minutes about the house and when they were done, I told Preston I'd call him later and ended the call.

Reaching out to me, she said, "Help me up?" I grabbed her hands and pulled her to stand. She stepped out of the tub, smoothed her hands over her pants, and walked out into the bedroom. "I think I feel a little slighted. You bought Mehki a full bed, complete with comforter and sheets and this is all I got?"

Chuckling, I said, "I figured you would want a less cartoonish bed set."

I went to kiss her again, but she ducked, spinning away from me and leaving the room. I followed her down the stairs into the living room. "Angel, what's going on?"

It took a while for her to answer me, but she finally turned to face me. "I've been thinking."

"About?"

"I heard you with Mehki the last time we were here."

I thought back to the conversation I'd had with Lil Man. "Okay?"

"He really loves you."

"I love him, too."

"I know. But I've been his one constant, I've protected him, taken care of him. And I have to continue to do that. Cooper, things between us feel too big for me right now."

My stomach tightened. "What does that mean exactly?"

"It means what I said. It's fine when we're together. We're in sync, we're having fun. But I don't like feeling like everything is going to come crashing down. I don't want to fall without a net."

The pieces were clicking rapidly, as everything started to make sense. Her behavior the last night we were together, the tears after we made love. She'd stayed away from me, and she'd kept Mehki away today.

"You can tell me I'm not," she rushed on. "But you haven't made a commitment to be a full-time presence at Prescott Holdings, even after you found out it was what your grandfather wanted."

"Angel, the situation is complicated. I own a whole company, not connected to my family's company."

"Exactly. You could decide tomorrow that you want to move back to Detroit. Where would that leave me? Where would that leave my son? He already loves you. He told you he wanted you to marry me and be his daddy."

So, she'd heard the *entire* conversation. Up until that point, I wasn't sure what she'd overheard. "I know."

"I can't risk his heart, Cooper. I can't stop protecting him because *I* hope for something you might not be ready to give us." A tear fell from her eye. I wiped it away with my thumb. "And I don't want you to feel obligated to be what we need. So, I think we need some space."

Everything was happening too fast. I needed to slow this down, I needed to figure out a way to fix it. "What if I don't want space?" I asked.

Her shoulders fell. "It's not your choice." She broke free from my hold and walked to the door. "I have to go. Bye, Cooper."

Then, she left me. And nothing would ever be the same again.

ANGEL

"IT'S GOING to be okay, sis." Tee rubbed my back. I'd cried nonstop the entire ride home, eventually stopping at a rest stop to get myself together, before I finished the drive. "You did what you thought was best."

"Do you think it was best?" I asked, desperate to find a reason to take it all back.

"I'm not Mehki's mother," Tee said. "You're not wrong for wanting to protect your son. From what you've told me, Cooper still hasn't even talked about moving to Rosewood Heights."

I'd gone over everything countless times. None of his friends and family thought he would stay in Rosewood Heights. I'd heard Dallas tell him to bring sweet tea home. I'd heard him tell Preston he wanted to be present for his company's new project. The times that I'd seen him with his siblings, I'd heard the jokes about him still being there. It almost felt like I was the last person to realize this couldn't go anywhere.

"Then, why do I feel like I fucked up, Tee?"

"I don't know."

"You always tell me not to overreact, not to jump to conclusions. I didn't give him a chance to prove me wrong."

"You heard him, you heard his family and friends."

"But my heart doesn't want to believe it. I was there, Tee. I spent time with him, I felt it. He didn't say the words, but I *felt* it."

"So, talk to him. Ask him. What did he say when you told him how you felt?"

I swallowed. I was so determined to get out of there before I broke down that I never told him how much I loved him. I'd kicked myself, too. In the end, though, I figured it was for the best. Because if I'd revealed myself him, opened myself up even more and he'd rejected me? I would've been devastated.

"I didn't tell him," I admitted softly.

"What?" Tee asked. "Why?"

"Because!" I explained my reasoning. "I can't…"

"Oh, sis." She leaned her forehead against my shoulder.

"I should have left him alone. I shouldn't have gotten involved with him in the first place. I never thought I'd fall in love again, but I couldn't help myself. He was too charming, too good, too smart."

"I've never been where you are. So, I can't pretend to know what you're going through. But I wish you would've just been honest with him, even if it didn't go like you hoped. At least, then, you would know you've done everything you could."

I wiped my face. "I don't want to regret my decision." *But I do.* "I feel like we didn't have enough time, I didn't get to see him through the different seasons. We didn't watch the fireworks, or go out on the water, or rake leaves, or play in the snow. Mehki didn't get to learn how to play basketball or use a hammer and nails."

Raising Mehki without Malachi had many challenges, but it was the moments we wouldn't have together that made me sad. And now I felt that familiar sting when I thought about Cooper.

"Cooper is not dead, sis." Tee sighed. "He's still alive. *You're* still alive. I think you need to talk to him. And let's start by reframing this entire situation."

I met her gaze. "How so?"

"You told him you needed space. Right?"

I nodded. "Yes."

"So in my view that leaves the door open. Take a few days, pack, and if you're still feeling the pull, call him."

"Mommie!"

I dabbed my eyes with a tissue, sucking in a deep breath and plastering on a smile for my son. Mehki barreled into the room and into my arms. I hugged him, resting my head against his. "Hey, baby," I said.

Mehki pulled away. "Grandpa bought me a Spider-Man book. I want to show it to Mr. Cooper. So he can see that Spider-Man is the best."

I glanced at Tee, who made a sad face. Then, I cupped Mehki's chin in my hands. I'd decided not to tell him about Cooper yet. Just in case Tee was right and there was still a chance we could make this work. "I'm sure he would love that."

Tee smiled, giving me an encouraging nod. "I agree."

"Hey, sweetie." My mother walked into the room and gave me a kiss on my cheek. "Hi, Tee. Sorry, we're late. Mehki had me running all day." She blew out a deep breath and handed me a black plastic bag.

"What is this?" I asked.

"Your mail," Mom replied. "I forgot to give it to you."

I frowned. My parents had collected my mail when I was in Rosewood Heights back in January for a few weeks. But I thought she'd given it all to me when I came back. "You already gave me my mail, mom."

"This is the first batch." She bit her thumb. "I had tossed in the back of the truck and forgot about it. It was hiding under a box. I hope there wasn't anything important in there."

I opened the bag and peeked inside. Pulling out a few pieces, I looked them over, tossing several in a throwaway pile on the floor. But one envelope stood out to me, the handwritten script very familiar. I peered at the return address. "Oh my God. This is from Aunt Lou," I announced, tearing it open.

Running my hand over the cursive, I read.

My Dearest Angel,

There is so much I never got to tell you, so I figured I'd write the big stuff down. I don't know that we'll ever see each other again, because I'm not well. Every day, I get a little weaker. But don't worry, I've lived a full, albeit controversial, life.

If I could boil my life down into three lessons that I can pass on to you, I would tell you to never be afraid to fall in love. I fell in love once. And, no matter where I am, I can never forget the feeling of being with Abraham. We were young and stubborn, but he mattered. Remember the portrait on the wall you used to stare at? He put that smile on my face, the joy in my heart. And even though our relationship didn't work out, and we both went on to marry other people, I never stopped loving him. So, take a chance on love again. It really is the best that life has to offer.

Tears fell down my face as I reflected on the portrait. The entire time, Cooper was right. His grandfather had loved my great-aunt. And he'd made arrangements to give her what she'd wanted, even on his deathbed.

I flipped to the second page.

Another thing. Please have fun. Life is hard enough without laughter. Lastly, spend some time on yourself. You won't be any good to Mehki if you burn yourself out. Trust me, I know. Pamper yourself. Read more. Sit in the sun. But not too much because you don't want to shrivel up like a prune. Wear your sunscreen.

I never had a daughter. But you were always the bright spot in my life. I love you.

Aunt Lou

Folding the pages, I cried softly.

Mehki climbed in my lap and hugged me. "Don't cry, Mommie."

I held his little head in my palm and let him comfort me. "I'll stop in a minute, babe."

Tee and my mother wrapped their arms around us,

and we stayed like that for a moment. Eventually, I pulled away. "Thanks." I grabbed another tissue and wiped my face. "I'm so glad you had this, Mom."

Mom dashed a tear from her own cheek. "I'm glad you got to know Aunt Lou the way you did. You can rest assured; she knew you loved her. And she loved you."

I nodded. "I know." I held the letter to my chest. "I know."

Chapter 10

COOPER

N*ever let your mistakes stop you from doing better.*

Once again, I'd fucked up. Angel left me because I was too chickenshit to say something to ask her to stay. I let her go because I couldn't tell her the truth. I watched her walk away, get in her car, and drive to a whole 'nother city because I didn't tell her I loved her.

After she drove away, I'd grabbed the tarantula and left. I didn't keep it, though. I made arrangements for the pet store to deliver it whenever they moved in. I spent a few days wallowing. But after I finished my second fifth of cognac, I tossed the liquor and hopped into action.

Granddad once told me to move in silence, so I turned off my phone and got to work. Now, I was ready to fix the shit I'd broken.

The ringing of the doorbell broke my momentum, and I tossed a few shirts in my suitcase and hurried to the door.

Pulling it open, I was surprised to see my brothers on the other side.

Frowning, I asked, "What the hell are y'all doing here?"

Dom pushed past me. "I got an SOS call from Dallas, through Ava. I called for reinforcements."

The rest of my brothers entered my condo. I closed the door and turned to them. "Why?"

"She said you were probably sprawled out on the floor, crying into a fifth of Hennessy." Mav plopped down on the leather sofa. "You don't look drunk, though."

"Because I'm not, dumb ass." I sat on my Lazy Boy.

"Everybody is just worried," Hunter said. "You haven't answered your phone, bruh. We wanted to make sure you were good."

I pulled out my phone and turned it on, cringing when I saw all the messages. "As you can see, I'm fine."

"Where's the cognac?" Mav asked. "I was prepared to have a few shots with you before Dom whooped your ass for falling off the grid again."

I glared at my youngest brother. "I threw it out."

Dom leaned forward, resting his elbows on his knees. "What the fuck is wrong with you, Coop?"

"I think what Dom is trying to say—"

"What the fuck is wrong with you needs no interpretation, Hunter."

"Nothing is wrong with me," I told them. "I had to get my shit together, and I couldn't do what I needed to do in Rosewood Heights. So I left."

"Because Angel left yo' ass," Mav said. "Dallas told me the story."

I made a mental note to cuss Dallas' ass out next time I saw her. "What did she tell you?"

Dom shook his head. "That you fucked up."

"She left you," Hunter added.

"All of that is true," I admitted. "She told me she needed space, so I gave it to her." *Temporarily*.

"I still don't know why anyone would throw good liquor out." Mav nudged Hunter. "He might be losing his mind."

"I'm not crazy," I said with a shrug. "I'm came here to pack because I'm moving. Throwing shit out comes with the territory."

Groaning, Dom rolled his eyes. "There you go again. Things don't go your way and you just walk away."

"Where exactly are you going?" Hunter asked.

"Home. To Rosewood Heights. To be near my family."

"Us?" Mav pointed at his chest.

I shot him an annoyed glance. "Not *you*, nigga. Angel. And Mehki."

Hunter grinned. "What?"

Smirking, Dom said, "About time you came to your senses. They're good for you."

"I know that. That's why I'm moving. I also talked to Dad." The call to my father wasn't long. I'd simply told him that I was moving back home and would start at Prescott Holdings in September. "Before you get too excited, I'm not making any promises. I'm still very invested in Prescott-Hayes Construction. I spent a lot of years building that company, and I'm not willing to walk away from it completely."

Hunter told me he understood. "At least, it's a start."

"Granddad's death changed everything for me," I admitted. In hindsight, I thought *he* knew it would.

I glanced at each of my brothers, recognizing the sadness in all of their eyes. Granddad had a different relationship with each of us. His absence would be felt forever. It didn't surprise me that his final wish for me had led me to realize *my* wish for myself. Restoring Louse Fox's home restored my faith, my heart. And I wouldn't walk away from it. I *couldn't* if I tried.

I stood. "I know y'all just flew here and everything to check on me, but I have to get on the road. I'm on a schedule."

Hunter laughed.

"So you're just going to let us come all the way here and not even feed us?" Mav asked. "Who does that?"

"Me," I said, matter-of-factly.

Dom slid off the couch and walked over to me. Clasping my shoulder, he said, "You did good. Angel is beautiful. I hope she takes your ass back. We don't need another repeat of the post-Ryleigh years. You're too old to be sad and pitiful."

I laughed, shoving him. "Get the hell away from me, man."

Hunter chuckled. "I still can't believe you thought you were being slick about that."

Surprised, I asked my twin, "You knew too, man?"

Nodding, Hunter shrugged. "Everybody knew, bruh. Like I said, you ain't slick."

Maverick emerged from the kitchen, sipping a bottle of water. I hadn't even realized he'd walked out of the room. "You really don't have *any* food."

"You know what?" I grabbed my phone and my wallet. "Let's go get something to eat."

"Finally," Mav said. "Your treat."

A couple of hours later, I said goodbye to my brothers, packed up my truck, and got on the road. On the way out of town, I made one more stop.

"Coop!" Dallas smacked me. "I said I would kick your ass on sight, but I'm too happy you're not dead from alcohol poisoning."

Preston gave me a dap. "I'm glad you came by, man. I was tired of the interrogation."

Preston was the only person who'd known of my plan to move. And only because I had to tell him because of our business. "Thanks for not telling my business." I looked at Dallas, then back at Preston. Then, back at Dallas. "What are you doing at Dallas' house anyway?"

"Leaving," Dallas said, pushing Preston out of the door.

"Right," I said. There was definitely more to the story, but I didn't have time to find out. "Listen, I can't stay. But I wanted to tell you in person. I'm moving to Rosewood Heights. Tonight."

Her eyes widened. "Because you're in love with Angel."

"Yes," I grumbled.

"I knew it!" Dallas hugged me, then she smacked me again. "That's for planning a move to whole 'nother state without telling me. You're lucky Charleston is a short flight away. Punk."

I smiled, pulling my friend into a hug. "Thank you, Dallas. You were right."

She looked up at me. "I'm right 99.999% of the time."

I snorted. "Yeah, I'm not agreeing to that. I have to go. I'll keep my phone on," I added before she could.

"Bye, bruh. We have that conference call Monday. We'll talk before then."

Preston nodded. "Good luck, bruh."

The next day I was standing in front of the Fox-*now*-Crawford home. I spotted Angel's car in the driveway, courtesy of Tee, who I'd called a few days ago to tell her my plans. Angel and Mehki weren't scheduled to move in for a couple of weeks. Tee agreed to talk Angel into showing Mehki the house earlier.

I grabbed a few key items from my car and walked to

the door. Before I could knock, Mehki swung the door open, ran out of the house, and jumped in my arms.

"Mr. Cooper!"

I held onto him a little longer than normal, relishing in the moment. "What's up, Lil Man?" I set him down on the ground and he immediately spotted my surprise.

"A tarantula!" he shouted, dropping to his knees and peering into the cage. He pushed his glasses up on his face. "Is this my pet?"

I bent low. "Yes."

"I can't wait to show it my room. Thank you for my bed and my Spider-Man blankets." He babbled on about the Avengers, protons, and the periodic table. All in under a minute and a half. "And Mommie is making grilled cheese sandwiches and tomato soup with Tee."

I rubbed the top of his head. "I'm glad you loved it. Where's Mommie?"

"Right here." I looked up to find Angel standing in the doorway, a soft smile on her lips. "I see you brought your little friend back."

I stood to my full height. "I thought you might like some company."

"Mr. Cooper brought me a tarantula. Now, Mommie, I won't let him crawl on you. I'm going to keep him locked away in my room."

"Please do," she said.

I couldn't tear my eyes away from her. She was stunning. Her hair was down today, her curls wild. She had on a pair of black jeans and a white t-shirt with the word *Boss* pressed on it. Her lips were bare and her eyes dark. Her brown skin glowed in the sunlight and I had to stop myself from reaching out to touch her.

Mehki slipped his hand in mine and tried to tug me forward. "Come on, Mr. Cooper."

I picked up the cage and let him "pull" me into the house. The house was still pretty much empty, aside from a few boxes and a foldable card table with four chairs.

"I had to improvise," she explained. "If we're going to stay here this weekend, we need a table to eat on."

"Good idea," I said. "I would've just spread a blanket on the floor and ate."

She laughed. "I can see you doing that."

Tee rounded the corner from the kitchen. She grinned when she saw me. "Cooper, you're here."

"What's up, Tee?"

"Nothing much. Just came to collect Mehki so he can come help me… pour some water."

Mehki pouted. "But I want to stay here with Mr. Cooper."

"I'm not going anywhere, Lil Man," I assured him.

His face lit up. "Really?"

"Promise."

Mehki and Tee disappeared, leaving me alone with Angel. "Hi," I said finally.

"Hi," she said. "What are you doing here, Cooper?"

I inched closer to her. Reaching out, I brushed a strand of hair out of her face. "I came to tell you something."

She searched my eyes. "Something good?"

I kissed her. And she let me. "I think so," I murmured against her lips. "But you have to decide."

"It's a good thing you're here because I have something to tell you, too."

"Can I go first?" I asked, not wanting to prolong anything. "I just…" I picked up her hands and kissed her knuckles. "I need to say this."

Nodding, she told me, "Permission granted."

Taking a deep breath, I said, "I don't need from space

from you. I already know I can't live another moment without you."

Her eyes filled with tears. "You can't?"

I shook my head. "I thought I'd never want Rosewood Heights to be my home again. But home is not just a place to lay my head. Home is *here*—" I placed her hand over my heart. "—with you and Mehki. And if you're here, I'm here."

Closing her eyes, she whispered, "Promise?"

"Promise." I brushed my lips against hers, enjoying her low moan. "I love you."

She sucked in a deep breath. "I love you, too."

I wiped the tears from her cheeks. "What did you want to tell me?"

Smiling, she said, "I actually only have one more thing to say."

"What is it?"

"Welcome home."

Epilogue

COOPER

Eight Months Later

A year ago, Granddad had told me to come home. It took a while, but Rosewood Heights was the home I didn't know I needed. Angel and Mehki had opened up my heart and set up residence there. I wouldn't trade *this* life for anything. And, today, I hoped to make it official.

I didn't move in with them, per se. But I was at the house every day, and most mornings. Angel was a stickler about overnights, especially after Mehki walked in on us getting it in on top of the Monopoly board.

After I convinced Angel she wasn't a bad mother, we decided to keep the overnights to a minimum—at least while Mehki was there. Which meant we'd gotten very creative with our attempts to have some… alone time.

Mehki was thriving in Rosewood Heights. He loved his

school and he loved the town. He'd recently joined the youth basketball league. Lil Man had a good hook shot. Angel and I agreed he'd found his sport.

"Cooper?" Mehki put his tarantula in its cage. He'd dropped the *mister* after they moved into the house. "Can we have a talk? Man-to-man?"

"Do you want to talk in here?"

"Sure." He walked over to the table in the corner. "Have a seat."

Smiling, I pulled out the little chair and sank down in it. When the chair nearly buckled under my weight, I decided it might be better to sit on the floor. I slid onto the carpet. "Is everything okay, Lil Man?"

He nodded. "I've been thinking."

"About what?"

"I'm seven-years-old now. I'm not getting any younger."

I covered my smile, trying to keep my serious face on. "Understandable."

"Mommie isn't either. She needs stability."

Unsure where this was going, I said, "Right. We all need stability."

"You come over every day. I see you kissing her all the time. When are you going to marry her?"

I leaned forward. "Actually, I was going to talk to you about that today." I pulled out the ring box I'd been carrying around all day and opened it.

His eyes widened. "That's a diamond."

"It is. I want to give it to Mommie."

"You're going to marry her today?"

Laughing, I said, "No. I want to propose to her today. But I need your help."

Mehki frowned, as if in deep thought. "I can be the best man."

"Naturally."

"And I can help make sure there are no spiders around. Mommie hates bugs."

"Good point."

"What else can I do?" he asked.

"I just need your permission," I said. "You're important to both of us, and I want to be sure you're okay with me marrying your mom, moving in, becoming your—"

"Daddy. You will be my new daddy."

I exhaled. I already felt like Mehki was my son, but I always choked up when *he* mentioned anything about me being his father. "Right," I croaked. "I'll be your daddy."

Mehki wrapped his arms around my neck. "I love you."

Closing my eyes, I held him close. "Love you, too."

He pulled back. "You have my permission. Can you go ask Mommie now?"

"Ask me what?" Angel walked into the room with two glasses of lemonade in her hands. "What are you two up to?"

"Cooper wants to ask you something," Mehki announced, a wide grin on his face.

"What is it?"

"Can you give me your hand, baby?" I held my hands out. "I think I might be stuck on the floor."

Laughing, she helped me up. She smiled. "I told you he needed a practical table, not this Spider-Man thing you bought him."

"It's cool," I argued. "But short."

"Exactly."

Mehki picked the ring box up off the floor and handed it to me. "Don't forget this," he said.

"Thanks, Lil Man."

Angel gasped, her hands flying to her cheeks. "Cooper, you… Oh." She looked at the box. "You're… Are you…?"

"Yes, baby. I am. You've made me the happiest I've ever been."

"What about me?" Mehki asked.

Chuckling, I said, "You, too." I met Angel's watery gaze again. "I love you so much. I want this life forever. I want my home to always be with you." I opened the box. "Marry me?"

"Oh, shit. That's huge." She clamped a hand over her mouth. "Sorry, Mehki." She grinned. "Yes!" She jumped in my arms and kissed me. "I can't wait to be your wife. I love you."

"Love you, too, baby."

Granddad told me sometimes time didn't heal all wounds. But standing here with my family, knowing that it was going to be like this forever, I could say sometimes it did.

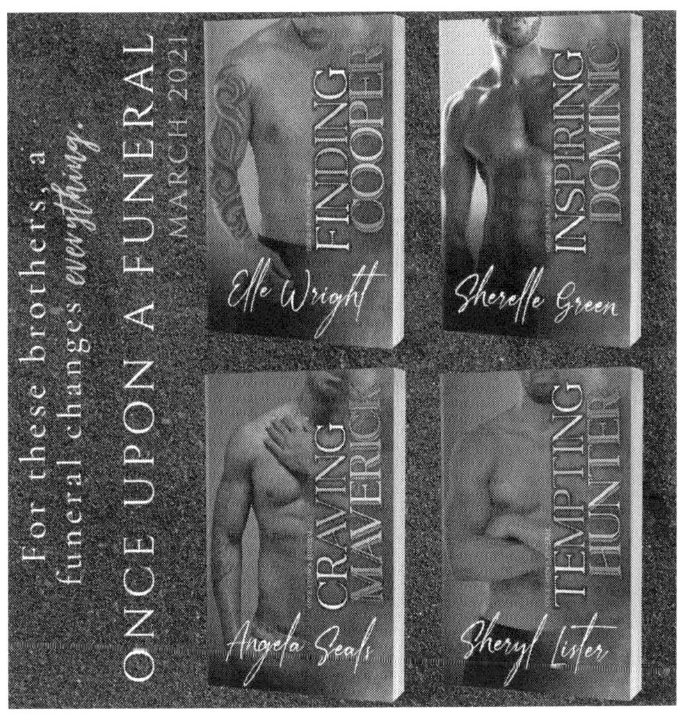

bit.ly/OUAFSeries

Check out the entire Once Upon a Funeral series:

When the powerful patriarch of the Prescott family dies, four brothers are challenged to return to Rosewood Heights and fulfill their grandfather's last wishes. With each of these compelling and complex men facing their inner demons, they must ask themselves if light can shine in the midst of tragedy and if home is truly where the heart is…

Finding Cooper by Elle Wright

Inspiring Dominic by Sherelle Green

Craving Maverick by Angela Seals

Tempting Hunter by Sheryl Lister

Her Little Secret

Sex therapist, Paityn Young, couldn't get much sex in her city. So she developed her own line of naughty toys to get the job done. Now, she's bringing her talent to LA, hoping to launch her new company. Only her new business consultant has her thinking about more than just her product line.

As a favor to his boss, Bishop Lang agrees to help Paityn develop her new business. The only thing he knows about her is that she's off limits, but the moment he sees her, he realizes staying away might be harder than he thought. And his own personal journey may take a backseat to the blossoming relationship developing between them.

Excerpt: Her Little Secret

WOMEN OF PARK MANOR

If Paityn could ban two words, *fuck* and *shit* would be it. One made her think of toilets. The other? Well, let's just say she didn't need to be reminded of something she hadn't been blessed to do in years. And for the last ten minutes, she'd listened to her sister string those same two words together in varying combinations.

"Girl! Enough!" Paityn shouted, cutting her sister off mid-curse. "Road rage is really a thing. Get help." Pulling two sets of new sheets out of the dryer, she walked into one of the spare bedrooms and dropped the bedding on the mattress.

"Shit, I need to vent," Blake yelled. "It's your fuckin' fault I'm in this predicament. Michigan traffic doesn't make me want to kill someone."

Unable to help herself, Paityn giggled at her younger sister's antics. "You're a mess."

"Hey, I can only be me," Blake said.

The loud blare of the car horn followed by another colorful curse had her shaking her head in amusement. Some things would never change. Trump was still an asshole, she still couldn't eat beans to save her life, and Blake Young still had a potty mouth.

"I'm hanging up," Paityn told her sister. "I have stuff to do before you get here."

When "the brats" told her they were coming for a visit during the Memorial Day holiday, Paityn was ecstatic. Since her cross-country move, she'd seen her sisters countless times thanks to technology. But air kisses and virtual hugs didn't replace real face-to-face contact.

"Paityn?" Bliss called through the phone. She noted the rasp in her baby sister's voice, as if she'd been sleeping. "Are you making something for dinner? I'm hungry."

"Yes, ma'am." She walked the other set of sheets to the third bedroom and dumped them on the bed. "I'm making reservations. At this new Cuban restaurant Rissa told me about."

"Damn," Bliss muttered. "Will you at least cook breakfast in the morning?"

"You're so greedy," Blake said. "You just ate a whole foot-long sub and half of mine."

"I can't help it," Bliss shouted.

"I'm starting to think you're only here because you want me to cook for you." Paityn hurried to the kitchen and opened the oven. The homemade peach cobbler she'd prepared was almost done, Blake's favorite.

"No, I'm here because I miss you," Bliss said, just as Blake shouted another obscenity at a driver.

"That's good to hear." She also checked the macaroni and cheese baking in the bottom oven. *My favorite.*

"I wish Dallas could have come," Bliss mused. "I tried to get her to cancel her plans."

Paityn lifted the top off the pot on the stovetop, stirring the mustard and turnip greens a bit before she turned down the heat. "I do, too. But I'm not mad at her for taking a vacation out of the country. It's about time." She glanced at the Instant Pot on the countertop, noting the remaining time on the pulled pork, Bliss' favorite.

The truth? She did have reservations for dinner and dancing. Tomorrow. But, tonight, she also wanted to spoil her sisters a little. And it had been a while since she'd cooked anything of substance.

Growing up the second oldest child of a world-renowned couple, known for mending relationships and teaching others to parent, had a unique set of challenges. Partly because it was hard to live in her parents' shadows, but mostly because there were eight of them. Yes, Stewart and Victoria Young had eight damn children—willingly and happily. Paityn was the responsible sister, the oldest daughter, always offering a plate of food, a hand to hold, and a shoulder to cry on.

"Duke is pissed you didn't invite him," Bliss said.

Paityn laughed, thinking of the phone call she'd received from her brother earlier that morning. "I didn't invite y'all."

"But you're glad we're here," Blake added.

"I am, but I'm hanging up. I gave the concierge your names, so you should be able to come up without any problems. Don't kill anybody, Blake. See you soon."

Paityn ended the call after her sisters screamed goodbye. Shaking her head, she turned the dishwasher on and poured a glass of wine. When the oven timer went off, she pulled the dessert out and set it atop the island. The smell of peaches and cinnamon wafted to her nose and she resisted the urge to taste the cobbler.

She scanned the notes she'd jotted down earlier that day. The clitoral cream she'd hoped to perfect had been harder than she originally thought. Between her work as a sex therapist and her science background, it should have been a no brainer. Yet, she'd failed to even achieve the big "O" for the first two batches she'd made. Biting her thumbnail, she pondered her choice of ingredients. Maybe she'd used too much sodium benzoate?

Paityn scribbled an idea on the notepad and eyed the prototype she'd created. It was the fifth dildo she'd created and, by far, the best. She couldn't wait to show Blake and Bliss, which was why it was out in the open and not in her makeshift office-slash-lab.

Once Paityn had decided every woman needed a big ass dick, the wheels started spinning and a business idea formed. Paityn knew there were other sex aids on the market, entire stores dedicated to the business of pleasure, but she'd jumped in anyway. Now she was preparing to pitch her brand of sexual enhancement products.

When her stomach growled, Paityn glanced over at the peach cobbler. *One spoonful won't hurt.* She grabbed a wooden spoon and scooped a heaping helping out of the pan. Before she knew it one bite turned into two. Then, three. *Oh my God.* Four.

Fortunately, the knock on the door interrupted her greedy moment. She licked the spoon as she headed toward the door. She'd figured it would be at least thirty minutes before her sisters arrived. The airport was less than fifteen miles away, but it almost always took more than thirty minutes to get there in the infuriating 405 traffic.

She wiped a hand against her black leggings and opened the door. "You're her—"

Only it wasn't Blake or Bliss at the door. It wasn't even Rissa. No, the very *male* visitor standing there, his fist poised to knock again, was someone she didn't know. But damn, he was someone she probably *should* get to know.

Swallowing, she plastered a grin on her face and hoped

she looked presentable. "Hi." When he didn't answer immediately, she swallowed. *Maybe the hottie is a creeper?* But it wasn't like she was in some random apartment building. The concierge didn't just let anyone come up to the top floor.

The stranger's eyes dropped to her mouth and she absently wiped it with her sleeve, hoping she didn't have peach cobbler crust on her face.

"Can I help you?" she asked.

He blinked and then blessed her with the sexiest smile she'd ever seen up close. Pretty white teeth, adorably deep dimples, and beautiful creases framing full lips.

"I'm sorry. My name is Bishop." He held out a hand, presumably for her to shake it.

Her gaze dropped to it, noted his long fingers and clean fingernails, but she made no move to touch him. *Not yet.*

"I work at Pure Talent," he continued. "Jax Starks told me about you."

Paityn's eyes widened. "Oh, yeah. Bishop Lang."

Why is my voice so high? Probably because when her godfather told her he wanted her to meet one of the best legal minds on his team, she'd assumed it was an old, graying grandfather. A man that golfed on his off days and spent weekends at some highbrow country club drinking Burnt Martinis or scotch on the rocks. Not this fine ass man with smooth dark skin and a body that made her want to sing, "Do me, Baby". Because she was sure he'd be able to handle the job in a way no one ever had before. *Focus, Paityn.*

"Yes, that's me." His tongue darted out to wet his lips. "I live in the building and figured I'd come up and introduce myself."

Unable to turn away, she nodded. "Right. I think Uncle Jax did tell me that."

Briefly, she wondered if this was even a good idea, considering she couldn't stop staring at him. How would she be able to concentrate on business? But she trusted her godfather's judgment because he had never failed her and always had her best interests at heart.

From an early age, Paityn learned that blood didn't make family. And it was because of relationships like the one her father and Jax Starks had. The two men had grown up near each other in Detroit, Michigan and had even pledged the same fraternity. They were brothers in every sense of the word, even though they were born to different parents. Jax was her godfather, but he was also her "uncle".

She finally stepped aside. "Come in."

He followed her toward the kitchen. "Peach cobbler." The low groan that followed hit her right in the gut—or lower. "Smells good."

She gulped down the rest of her wine and dropped the wooden spoon into the sink. "I'm making dinner for my sisters." She turned the greens off and tried to recall everything her godfather had told her about Bishop. Clearly, she'd missed some things that he'd said. "I thought you were going to be out of town until next week?"

"I got back a little early."

Paityn leaned against the counter, meeting his intense gaze once again. "Cobbler?" she asked.

He looked down at the dessert and swallowed visibly. Nodding slowly, he said, "No."

Paityn frowned, surprised at his answer. Normally, a nod meant yes. "You sure? Because you look like you want some."

"I'm sure." He glanced at the pan again, before he looked up at her.

Tilting her head, she studied him. Something was preventing him from eating her cobbler. Did she want to know what? *Or who*? The need to know more welled up inside her. *It's the nature of my job to ask questions*. It wasn't his arms. Or the muscles stretching against the t-shirt he wore. The fact that he may be eating someone else's pie didn't bother her either. Well, not really.

Instead of probing further, she decided a change of subject was best. "Uncle Jax tells me you work in the business development department," she said. "But what else should I know?" Okay, so her attempt to sound professional came out more sultry than businesslike.

"What do mean?" he asked.

Clearing her throat, she added, "Because if we're going to work together, I'd like to learn a little more about your ass." Her eyes widened. "I mean, your experience?"

He chuckled. "I can give you the long version, or the short version."

Hello, sexual innuendo. She really did need to get some. Everything about this man and this interaction made her mind sink to the gutter. Paityn scratched her neck. "How about we start with where you're from?"

"Long Beach."

She opened the refrigerator and pulled out two bottles of water and offered him one. "Law school?"

"Berkeley." He took the water and twisted off the cap. "I've worked for the agency for fifteen years, and I've been instrumental in negotiating several business deals for agency clients. Jax has also entrusted me with many of his personal business matters."

"Good. What has he told you about me?"

His mouth curved into a smile. "He mentioned you were important to him and that I should take care of you."

She bit down on her lip. "I mean, about my business idea."

"Only that you were a sex therapist looking to start a new venture."

Paityn grinned, pleased that he didn't seem uncomfortable with her occupation like some men. "That's true. Did he tell you anything else?"

Bishop raised a brow. "No. I assume you will tell me the details."

"Right. I'll send you the draft of my proposal." She slid her notebook over and jotted down a note to herself. "I probably should have done this as soon as he gave me your email address, but I didn't want to interrupt your vacation. I know we always say we won't check emails on vacation, but we always do."

Ha barked out a laugh. "I don't disagree with that."

"Let me know when you're free to meet." She closed the notebook. "I have appointments during the day, but I'm usually free in the evenings." Paityn conducted her sessions online, via video chat or text therapy, which she'd found to be a great alternative to in-office therapy. Most of her clients loved the convenience and it allowed her to work from the comfort of her home, wherever that was.

"I'll check my calendar and get back to you. I have your numbers."

"Great. You'll have an email tonight. Not that I don't think you wouldn't read my proposal before we meet, but you definitely should. And preferably not in the office. In front of people."

The last thing she wanted was for a picture of her prototype to flash across his screen while he had someone in his office. That would be embarrassing, for him and for her.

Bishop frowned. "Why do I feel like I should be scared?"

Paityn laughed. "Because you should." She waggled her eyebrows.

"Now, I'm curious. Maybe you should give me a hint?"

"I would, but—" A knock on the door interrupted her explanation. "Excuse me. I have to get the door."

She ran to the door and opened it. Before she could say anything, Blake and Bliss surrounded her, hugging her tightly. Paityn wasn't overly emotional, but it felt good to hug her sisters, and she held on for longer than normal.

Finally pulling back, she smiled at the twins, noting the tears standing in Bliss' eyes. She brushed her cheek. "Don't cry."

"Please don't." Blake rolled her eyes. "It hasn't even been a month. Get it together."

"Leave me alone." Bliss elbowed Blake. "At least I don't have a black heart."

Paityn giggled. "Get in here." She pulled one of the rolling suitcases inside. "Are you hungry?"

Bliss patted her stomach. "You know it."

"I thought you weren't cooking," Blake said.

Paityn led them around the corner into the open living room area. "You know I wasn't going to let you come here without making your favorites."

"So, no Cuban food?" Blake asked. "Because I had my mouth set… Oooh wee. This place is gorgeous. Floor-to-ceiling windows, stunning artwork. And I love the color scheme. Everything just flows. Uncle Jax is doing big things."

Bishop glanced up from his phone and stood. "Hi."

Blake bit down on her thumbnail. "And apparently so are you," she muttered under her breath.

"Who is that, sissy?" Bliss whispered.

"And tell me he has a brother," Blake added.

Paityn rolled her eyes. "Shut up." She introduced them to Bishop. "He's an attorney at Pure Talent and he's helping me with my business."

"Oh, so you're helping her with the Big Ass D?" Blake asked, a wicked gleam in her eyes.

Bishop blinked. "Excuse me?"

Paityn glared at Blake. "He doesn't know about that yet," she said between clenched teeth. Leave it to her little sister to embarrass the hell out of her. "I'm sorry, Bishop. Don't mind her."

"Is that peach cobbler?" Blake asked.

"Yes," Bliss answered from the kitchen. She lifted the top off the pan. "And there's greens. And it smells like pulled pork. Yum."

Paityn shrugged when Bishop met her eyes. "Sisters."

"Right," he said. "I should probably get going, let you visit with your sisters. We'll talk."

"I'll walk you out."

He waved her off. "You don't have to."

"I do." Paityn walked him to the door. "Thanks for stopping by. I'm looking forward to working with you." She finally reached out to shake his hand.

When their palms met, she couldn't help but notice how the contact flooded her with warmth, from the tips of her fingers to her shoulders and throughout her body.

"It's good to meet you, Paityn." His husky, low voice made her want to lean into him.

She didn't, though. Slipping her hand from his, she nodded. "Right."

"I'll talk to you soon."

She nodded again. Because apparently she couldn't form any words.

Once he was safely outside the door, she exhaled. If every interaction with him ended with a handshake that somehow felt more like a kiss or a tender caress against her bare skin… *I'm definitely in trouble.*

Recommended Reading

MEET THE YOUNG FAMILY

If you enjoyed meeting Cooper's friend, Dallas Young, you'll be happy to know she has a lot of siblings! And they are so much fun!

First up, Paityn Young found everlasting love in my Park Manor Novella, HER LITTLE SECRET. The twins, Blake and Bliss made their first appearance in her story. I also gave a quick introduction to most of the siblings and their parents.

Blake Young appeared again as Ryleigh's friend in my Once Upon a Baby Novella, BEYOND EVER AFTER.

And then there is Duke!!!! Duke Young burst onto the scene in my Pure Talent Novels, THE WAY YOU TEMPT ME and THE WAY YOU HOLD ME. And he stole the show.

If you're interested in meeting the Young Clan, I would recommend you start with the above books. Because the Young in Love Series is coming very soon!

www.ellewright.com

Coming Spring 2021

IT'S NOT ME, IT'S YOU

Known to her peers as the The Break-Up Expert, Blake Young suddenly finds the man that makes her question everything she thought she knew.

Also by Elle Wright

Contemporary Romance

Edge of Scandal Series

The Forbidden Man

His All Night

Her Kind of Man

All He Wants for Christmas

Once Upon a Series

Beyond Forever (Once Upon a Bridesmaid)

Beyond Ever After (Once Upon a Baby)

Jacksons of Ann Arbor

It's Always Been You

Wherever You Are

Because Of You

All For You

Wellspring Series

Touched By You

Enticed By You

Pleasured By You

Pure Talent Series

The Way You Tempt Me

The Way You Hold Me

The Way You Love Me

Distinguished Gentlemen Series

The Closing Bid

Women of Park Manor

Her Little Secret

Carnivale Chronicles

Irresistible Temptation

New Year Bae-Solutions

One More Drink

Historical Romance

DECADES: A Journey of African American Romance

Made To Hold You (The 80s)

Suspense/Thriller

Basement Level 5: Never Scared

Connect with Elle!

Subscribe to my Newsletter
New Releases, Upcoming projects, and Freebies!

On Facebook,
Join my cocktail lounge for exclusive updates, drink recipes, and lots of fun!
bit.ly/EllesCocktailLounge

Visit my website: www.ellewright.com

Email me at info@ellewright.com

facebook.com/ellewrightauthor
twitter.com/LWrightAuthor
instagram.com/lwrightauthor
amazon.com/Elle-Wright/e/B00VMEWB78

Acknowledgments

First, I want to thank God for loving me.

To my husband and children, thank you for being my home, my everything. I love you so much.

To my sista friends… You ladies are amazing! Love y'all!

A special shout-out to the amazing readers , bloggers, and awesome writers that I've met on this journey. Thanks for your support. I appreciate you!

About the Author

There was never a time when Elle Wright wasn't about to start a book, wasn't already deep in a book—or had just finished one. She grew up believing in the importance of reading, and became a lover of all things romance when her mother gave her her first romance novel. She lives in Michigan.

Connect with Elle!

www.ellewright.com

info@ellewright.com

Made in the USA
Columbia, SC
02 April 2021

35496920R00105